We had been so good together, then suddenly it was all over with no explanation...

The *Dear John* on the dresser read that she needed time away to reflect on the ongoing genocide of our emotions. She was exhausted from the reviled arguments and the chaos in our life. By that, she meant my stubbornness and my unwillingness to open up.

Our love had fallen from grace amid this ineluctable madness. But it wasn't until our thoughts ceased to be in concert that her resolve to leave had cemented.

In a vision, dated as far as the birth of her emptiness, she had waited for her soul mate by the waterfalls and had recognized in me the face of that mystical person when she first laid eyes on me—she often reminded me in our quiet moments. Love gave us such invincibility that failing was never in the forecast.

Yet she had gone back to Duluth.

For the next three weeks, I stayed at a squalid motel. The very sight of our empty home was too much of a strain to confront. My world had crumbled apart, and along with it our life.

A life that had freed our souls from loneliness.

One morning, I was driving, from ward to ward, to an unknown destination for the sake of escaping, with only her in my thoughts and the fresh air as my voice of reason. Uncertain of what the future would bring, my heart was racing fast.

In the end, all roads led me back to our home. I stopped there for a moment to savor the happiness of a past life. Memories of her were never too far from my mind. I imagined her standing by the door, waiting for me. Coming home to her was the best part of the day, impatient as always to see her beautiful smile that had illuminated my whole world ever since.

With my face pushed against the window screen, the chanting of my heart turned into languid beats. I lingered for her caress and found no deliverance from loneliness. In the center of my misery, faith was all I had left in my possession to keep my head above water.

In that incongruous moment, I took courage at hand and unlocked the main door. Inside the house, the air was redolent of the sillage of her perfumes and unfettered more sorrow within. I resented the implication that she left so unceremoniously. As hard as it was then to just formulate of such eventuality, a consequence too frightening to even contemplate, now it had become a reality.

I drove off.

Tristan falls into the grip of despair and alcohol abuse as the result of betrayal, eventually understanding that his relationship fallout might not be the root cause of his demise. Before this unsurmountable pain, he is forced to face reality for the first time, having lived in denial for years. At every twist and turn of this journey, he collects pieces of the puzzle that would unravel the mystery of his life. With each discovery, it becomes clear that he has been living a lie all along, and that the people he most trusts have turned their backs on him. The truth finally comes to light when he finds the love of his life, only to realize that their past traumas will be detrimental to their happiness. Alone again, his rehabilitation, now in jeopardy, will depend on the excavation of his true self. *The Veil of the Soul* explores the resilience of the human spirit and shows another side to the suffering inherited from the Vietnam War.

KUDOS for *The Veil of the Soul*

In *The Veil of the Soul* by Jess Lee Jalao, Tristan moved with his family from Laos to France after the Vietnam War when he was just a child. From France the family eventually moved to the US. Tristen's life seems to be a series of painful and traumatic events, culminating in his desperate thoughts of suicide. He's a troubled man, beaten down by life, betrayed those both family and those he thought were his friends and loved one, leaving him to wonder about the meaning of it all. While the subject is not particularly comfortable, Jalao handles it with sensitivity and compassion—a touching, poignant, and thought-provoking read. ~ *Taylor Jones, The Review Team of Taylor Jones & Regan Murphy*

The Veil of the Soul by Jess Lee Jalao is the story of a man whose existence has been nothing but pain, beginning with his life as a young child in Laos. His father was in the Laos Army under the auspices of the CIA, who conducted a "secret war" in Laos. Then the US pulled out of Laos in 1975, leaving their former "allies" to face the consequences of retaliation by the totalitarian government bent on revenge. So, after unthinkable sacrifices in an effort to preserve freedom, his family fled to France. Life there was not much better. Not only was he in a foreign country struggling to make his way in a world he didn't understand, his family was large and what attention he got was mostly negative, if not actual abuse—one of those stories that make you say, "And I thought I had problems." Jalao tells a powerfully moving and thought-provoking tale that puts daily struggles into perspective and highlights the sacrifices made by those driven out of their homelands by circumstances beyond their control and how long ranging the consequences can be. It's a book not easily forgotten. ~ *Regan Murphy, The Review Team of Taylor Jones & Regan Murphy*

ACKNOWLEDGMENTS

"Do. Or do not. There is no try." ~ Yoda

Nobody has been more important to me in the completion of this project than my daughter, Evelyn, the true love of my life, who never allows me to despair when all is darkness. She is the pillar of my sanity and the spark that ignited the firestorm within, wise beyond her years. I owe her everything.

A debt to my entire family, and especially my nieces and nephews—too many to mention and too few in this world.

A special shout out to Timothy Lanier, my brother from another mother, who gave me unconditional support from the beginning—as long as I provided the booze.

I am grateful for my cousin, Meng Vue, who digitally enhanced the artwork of the cover.

Many thanks to Lauri Wellington for acquiring my work and the Black Opal team, Faith and Jack and whomever else was involved in this project, whose contribution made the book an even better read.

Last but not least, a gargantuan *merci beaucoup* to my dear friend, mentor and editor, Bonnie Hearn Hill, for the bona fide guidance and without whom none of this would have happened so soon, if at all, for that matter.

Believe.

ACKNOWLEDGMENTS

The Veil of the Soul

Jess Lee Jalao

A Black Opal Books Publication

GENRE: WOMEN'S FICTION/FAMILY LIFE/WAR

THE VEIL OF THE SOUL

Cover Design by Jess Lee Jalao

Print ISBN: 978-1-626948-03-7

First Publication: NOVEMBER 2017

Published by Black Opal Books http://www.blackopalbooks.com

DEDICATION

To my parents, May Ly Yang and Lytoukao Jalao.

Chapter 1

La Bella Mariana

D*eath, a much sweeter retreat, I acquiesce.*

Another miserable night gone by, spent in the company of a bottle of vodka while my head throbs in excruciating pain. Disoriented, I wake to the penetrating yet soothing reverberation of a symphony orchestra composed of larks and cicadas that invokes, strangely, the music of Bach. In paramount enthusiasm, they celebrate the universe while another day slowly arises amidst a pleasant lassitude of freshness.

Joyful disturbance well-appreciated, I must say.

To my consolation, I have managed to get, at last, a few hours of rest—a remarkable accomplishment, considering the current circumstances in my life.

Gradually, the sun percolates into the grandeur of the milky spotted welkin and unleashes vigorously its scorching rays against the surface of my body. It appears as if they depict the singing poison-tipped arrows of the mischievous angel that aim to pierce through the frail cuirass of my heart.

In a ripple effect, I feel terrible aches along my stiffened neck and spine from the night spent in the back seats of my van. With tears still welling in my eyes, my appearance resembles far too well that of a bloodthirsty creature unable to find peace in sleep. I've spent countless white nights on account of my sorrow, obfuscated in a caricature of madness.

As I lay here, enfeebled, rigor mortis, as it seems, triumphantly encroaches toward the last standing capital of hope inside of me.

Like dust in the wind, the vestige of my life has burnt to a cinder, and even my home has been taken away. The clothes on my back are all that's left of a lost paradise where happiness once reigned in a totalitarian regime.

Or so, I believed.

My life, which had been, hitherto, an array of tribulations, has reached its expiration date. As much as I wish for the turmoil to vanish within a simple blink of the eye, reality resurfaces instantly. And along comes pain—inconsolable, Challenger Deep, abysmal pain. At times, I retrieve memories of happier moments, warped by delusion, in a vain attempt to convince myself that the course of my life has not been derailed out of its natural trajectory.

I imagine a warm embrace and a soul-healing meal still await me home.

With a shudder of remorse, I concede that my life had passed me by, unnoticed, in giant leaps. Wallowing with eyes wide open, I contemplate salvation through the tarnished windshield as though waiting for a divine apparition. But help would not materialize into such a shape and form, and surely the bitterness of my relationship fallout would not dissipate either. As a swelling torrent in monsoon season, the ingression of the darkness has finally lacerated through my shield and demands my capitulation before the intensity of the pain.

Defeated, I accept my morbid fate in desolation, but the prevalent pain is not nearly as forgiving. It engulfs severely further with each memory that converts into rancor and then, at the finishing line, suffering. Likened to a living organism, the pain feeds on my soul and hunts for the remnants of my life energy.

Life is mercilessly cruel and love so unkind, when all I've ever wanted is to love and be loved in return.

Being a neophyte in the matters of the heart has finally caught up with me. Along with love, comes inevitably pain. To the utmost degree, I have unwittingly heeded little attention to that simple concept, perhaps due to indifference, or even impertinence.

But in this darkest hour, I have plenty of time to reflect upon the misfortunes of my life. Love and pain represent the two facets of the same coin, although I have been solely dealing with the undesirable side of late.

All of a sudden, the world becomes a cold place through the lens of a broken man. This pain doesn't show any preferential treatment to anyone.

No one is spared.

A long silence imposes, the same sort that creeps at a funeral, as if I am mourning my own death, and sure enough, I am. I proclaim myself dead for I stop living from within. After a slew of defeat, it appears that I have inherited the genetic encoding of a life that excludes any abeyance from suffering.

From the moment I was old enough to understand life, I was cautioned not to let my emotions get in the way of making radical decisions. Apparently, I'd failed miserably. As if immune to good advices, I made poor choices and the situation has only worsened with the years. Throughout my life, I've been known to have an obstinate nature. That man is no more today.

My will had been shackled down, and my equilibrium shaken.

Although my mind represents the single most valuable tool I possess, it has not operated rationally due to the deceptive impulses of my heart.

The once incandescent light of my faith is now just a blurred flare incapable of sending signals to warn against any forthcoming danger. Like a wave washed ashore, that light slowly vanishes before my eyes.

Desperately, my sanity hangs by a filament as madness corrodes the very core of my humanity.

In truth, I wanted to be left alone in quiet solitude while awaiting the ultimate anesthesia. Marred with the spirit of a man at the end of his rope, I resorted to the physical by perforating holes in walls bare-knuckled with intent to expunge the emotional distress.

The plan did not work in my favor, however. All those emotional excavations left my heart with the semblance of an archeological dig.

In all my years, I have never felt anything so destructive. But in all honesty, I started to enjoy every bit of it lately. Far more frequently, I find appetite in wanton destruction to appease the anger, even for just a scintilla of relief.

Pain is so close to pleasure, indeed. A believer, I've become.

Containing my pain, in any way possible, has become the sole objective, an insane occupation yet a necessity. Similar to those descending moments right before falling asleep, there is no point to intellectualize anything anymore. Perhaps something in me needs this pain.

Fermented in an accrued inward violence, I surrender to the magnitude of my suffering. I am tired of feeling it, breathing it, bleeding it, and especially fighting it. Could it be the preamble to an ill-fated life of misery?

I start to question the very merit of living.

Over time, my silent screams only resonate to amplify further the distress within. Secluded deeper in my failure, the nicotine and the alcohol become my only confidants as the tendrils of fumes desecrate every space I occupy.

Ironically, a liquor-breathed man told me the other day that I would die soon should I prolong this harmful lifestyle. Showing total indifference at first, I kept a straight face. Then sold to sins, I faked a grin and agreed to the nuance that I would die in dignity, whereas, years from now some caffeine-charged care nurse would be tube-feeding him and wiping his derriere. So maybe, for once, my choice of action was not as inept after all.

We laughed, at his expense.

After a series of phantasmagoria I think of the Tin Man who wished for a heart while I lie here trying to rip mine out of its thoracic cage. I snigger foolishly to myself in derisive dissension. If only the dummy knew the consequences, without any doubt he would decline from acquiring of one. Better yet, if he could see through my misery, he would understand that the curse of being human is to feel.

And to feel comes with a price. Pain.

Alone in a tumult of emotions, I am imbued with a cascade of crisis and bleed the bitterness of betrayal. For the wounds are so profoundly entrenched, it would certainly take ceaseless cajoling to seam the scars.

Before this pillage of my emotions, I am angry at God for this unshakable unrest. Is there a reason behind all this? I implore. Although I must confess, I have never set foot in a worship establishment of sort. Forthrightly, I condemn my parents for my birth and appeal for restitution from being born.

I was told that seclusion brings either madness or greatness. I agree with the former, in this case misery would not feed into creativity.

In some respects the situation is far worse than it seems. The eradication of my relationship has taken a tremendous toll on me. Not for a minute have I envisioned that my life would turn into such a dramatic way. At one point, I was certain that I had finally found the love that would last me a lifetime—an eternity.

Upon further reflection, all I perceive is the soiled portrait of a malleable-minded man who spent great exertion in helping others but sadly never received any guerdons for his gestures.

As I step out of myself, the darkness continues to seduce my soul toward the portals of madness, in gradual attrition. All I can hear are the flouts of my foes. I discern contentment in the complicity of their eyes as I fall. I have been stomped upon, my dignity obliterated. They had stripped me out of the only thing that is meaningful to me. Love.

The suddenness of the situation had not allowed me to prepare for this brute transition. I had been defeated in a battle I had not engaged myself in. Disarmed, I can't infuse my strength fast enough with the proper ingredients to emerge from this immense sea of agony. From one pocket of air to the next, I am struggling for a breath without any direction or guidance, and most important, without any faith to moor my angst to a palpable solace.

To my doom, I have underestimated the depth of impact of the pain.

Over the course of this whole ordeal, my resiliency had been reduced to velleity. For that matter, balance will not be restored any time soon. Subjected to an indigestive appetite in my mouth, I am still nibbling the harsh reality of what's left of my life. Although I have endured breakups before, never was I exposed to this level of pain. Perhaps, for the first time, I have felt a sense of completeness with this person.

Now that all that's precious is lost begins the dreadful descent back to the terrestrial orbit—needless to be a clairvoyant to prophesy a crash landing.

All my dreams are shattered. A simple man, I never expected much. All I wanted was a simple life under the azure of the sky. Instead, my world turned into a landscape bereft of all the enrapturing excitements and the people that matter to me.

All is sure to fall as I careen through dangerous territories, deep into darkness.

At last, the combination of the pain and the depression has succeeded in their role of destruction. Must have

I committed a horrendous act in my past life to be excluded from happiness in this one? I wonder.

Sore at heart, I hold myself in contempt for being so weak.

My entire world is in peril from the crushing blows of the agony that dictate my every move. I had preached to others not to give in to bitterness, yet a true Pharisee, I am the first one to relinquish such moral claim. In my defense, I'm certain anyone would understand if they were to walk in my shoes.

Deep inside, I am undignified by such a double-standard on my part.

For quite some time now, I have been embracing defeat, hoping for a quick exit. In so doing, I was in thrall to the pain. At this point, nothing is relevant anymore.

And, it sure doesn't matter.

I remain cold inside.

Discouraged by the apathy I've shown toward my own rehabilitation, my family and friends stopped helping me altogether. They have labeled me a lost cause. They had exhausted their efforts, all of which that could have been done within their power, before accepting that I have opted to walk the plank. And like a beaten naval fleet, they sailed off thousands of nautical leagues away from the maritime storm within me as I face the penal colony.

At first impression, Tough Love was thought to be the motive, but I soon realize it was a cellophane-case of abandonment. They mean business this time. In their eyes, I am as good as dead, and it is just a matter of time before they bring me flowers—black tulips by preference, if anyone were to ask.

Even Maman did not cry. She never did much, at least not in front of me and aloud.

And here I am today, alone as I have wished for all along, kneeling before the hypertension that's skyrocketing at terminal velocity to a near stroke or even heart attack probability. Obliged finally to comply with reality, I face the undeniable choice between life and death. Dying would mean the end of the agony whereas living to endure this pain most indefinitely.

Despite the fact that I am still fairly young, my body would not withstand the abuse much longer. The languid rhythm of my heart rate palpitation toward the flat line stage is a clear indication of that reality. In this darkest hour, the pain of an entire life comes upon me with fierce determination to sink me in, once and for all.

But peculiarly, my mind still manifests with some sort of resiliency—a last fight in me. Absurd as it sounds, I need a reason to live.

My daughter.

No one could have doctored the festering internal wounds but her. Awash with self-pity, I nearly omit her well-being. What has possessed me to be so self-absorbed and jeopardize her entire life?

Most issues in our existence are matters of degree,

and this, without question, is the lowest point I've fallen to.

Cold sweats crawl out of my skin.

Although the after-effects of this emotional holocaust are foreign to my comprehension, it seems my survival instinct has laid groundwork for spiritual healing. It had ignited in me a need to understand this vitriolic anger that has turned into self-destruction.

The next logical step would be to dig my way up. Quite elementary, that is, if one's mind were in the right place.

From what I take of all this, life doesn't necessary need a purpose nor to be devoid of one. In this case, however, I will argue that life isn't the focal point of the matter, but the manner of living it rather. This, I'm confident, constitutes the foundation for personal enlightenment.

To repair the faults of my mind, I must conduct a thorough psychological assessment to ascertain the root causes of the cruxes of my life. Expeditiously, I search deep within my soul for answers before doomsday occurs.

And so, there goes the story of my life thus far…

Chapter 2

Until the Whistle Blows

Flee, my children, flee this godforsaken country—flee."

A few years after Grandpa escaped from the concentration camp, the toxicants that the Vietcong had injected into his body and the daily low dosage of fell poison added to his nourishment finally claimed his last breath. My parents witnessed each step of his physical transmogrification, not a pretty sight said anyone in our immediate entourage whom could not bear their eyes upon him long enough. His flesh dried on the bones, the color of his skin smeared to ashen, and toward his last days, his emaciated frame resembled nothing but an empty carapace.

The story of his escape had been told innumerably. Struggling for each breath, he ran light as the wind with a band of detainees and rested only little from fear of being caught again. They moved swiftly but silently in the thick jungle, and that might've saved them from the demented search dogs that ferreted about for their scents long into the moonlit darkness. Before the break of dawn, the barking finally faded into silence behind their quickened footfalls.

Deep in the humidity of the dense vegetation, they ate roots, bamboo shoots, critters, and just about anything they put their hands on—even those damned canines if the occasion had offered itself. They quenched their thirst from puddles of mud left by the previous rain and kept going restlessly through an ocean of trees and exuberant green foliage that seemed to never end.

Some perished before reaching a safe ground, their wounds too deeply ingrained in their souls, their faith dimmed by fear and exhaustion weighing in each step. Five, in all, had succumbed among the handful that had escaped, their bodies laid to rest without proper burial and left to decompose in putrid smell of decay at the mercy of ravenous scavengers. To each one of them belonged a story to tell their families on how valiantly they stood before falling, unsung heroes they were. In their last request, usually along with a medallion, an old watch, a picture or anything at all with a sentimental value attached to it, they implored Grandpa to take to their beloved ones—a task that none wanted but was obliged to honor compulsorily.

At home, a commemorative inscription had been rendered in Grandpa's honor with an empty coffin beneath, a major contretemps for worms and maggots. The family mourned his death several weeks into his capture. His return was termed doubtful and ceased to convey any possibility in their minds. They knew all too well the inhumane treatments of prisoners of war in these places. Few, if any, have ever returned.

But there he was, after seven long months in that hell hole condemned as a slave, standing in front of his own home that had remained untouched, brick for brick, despite that war-crazed period of time. He stood immobile against the main door, not knowing whether to announce himself or to let someone else do the job to ease up the tension of his unprecedented return.

On the other side of the frail door, the day had barely started, and no commotion could be heard. Grandma, whose grief so consuming had sprouted many white hairs, was sitting alone in her corner, as usual, with the blueprint of anxiety delineating each wrinkle of her face. She had not slept much since his capture, and everyone was concerned about her diminishing health.

Little did she know that her prayers had been answered. In the stillness of the early morning, the barking of the family's dog betrayed his presence. Instantly, a strange sensation bombinated inside Grandma's head.

She rushed to the door to find a revenant standing right before her eyes. She squinted against the morning glare many times over, out of disbelief, before thrusting herself forcibly forward to greet the man who had haunted her nights all these months. But he was far from the man he had been. Half the meat on him was gone. They stumbled on the pebbly, reddish ground.

My father heard Grandma's screams of joy and ran to the door to meet his returning father. They all held onto each other and cried. Although she felt the warmth of his arms around her, she pressed tightly against him for reassurance that he was truly alive.

Those seven months in captivity had completely transformed the man inside into a complete stranger. He looked whole but came back in bits and pieces. Seemingly seeking for a breath, his eyes in constant search for safety here and there reflected fear, his speech, at a chelonian pace.

Many years after his miraculous return, death stared him in the eyes again, this time, the end of the spiral of life a sure thing to befall. All food consumed came out in bloody vomit and diarrhea. His demise inevitable, he congregated the family and relayed his patriarchal reign onto my father and in a last slothful gasp pled, "Flee my children, flee this God forsaken country—flee." Then he plunged into darkness.

In a sinister end, that era of war claimed the life of my grandfather as he died the very same year I was born into this abominable world. Due to this unfortunate timing, I had never known him, and that event undoubtedly remained one of the greatest tragedies of my life. Grandpa was a designated civil judge, and because of his social status was he captured and tortured by communist culprits. Though he escaped the concentration camp, his life was scripted to end prematurely from the long and agonizing after effects of the lethal injections.

As for my father, he enlisted in the army at the age of seventeen. Soon after, he was conscripted into a special guerilla unit under the auspices of the CIA to fight off the negative aggression of the North Vietnamese forces into Laos and the neighboring neutral territories. That period of warfare is also known as the CIA's *Secret War* in Laos, which aimed to preserve strategic locations to the sacrifices of many for the freedom of a few.

My father's battalion was assigned to retrieve downed American pilots when their aircraft crashed deep in the jungles, although the specific part of his mission was to intercept North Vietnamese military supplies along the Ho Chi Minh trail that incised through a portion of Laos. Father, a simple Hmong man, was later promoted to the rank of Captain in the Royal Lao Army and served in that capacity until the war was officially over.

After the US pulled its troops out of Laos in 1975, an estimated 100,000 and counting of my countrymen, the Hmong people, had died. Those who survived became the targets of retaliation to genocidal tyrants.

To this day, the world has turned a blind-eye on their sacrifices that directly contributed in the protection and preservation of freedom, and their laudable actions have been left unmentioned in history books.

After spending little over a year in a rudimentary Thai refugee camp, my family was evacuated to the southern region of France, the Midi-Pyrénées, away from the atrocities of that war-torn part of the world. Overnight, we disembarked on new shores, in hopes of finding freedom and a better life.

My father's first and only choice was America, due to his direct involvement with the CIA, but his wish was not granted. All the Hmong soldiers from the alliance and civilians alike were abandoned to die. And because the situation for officers of his rank was punishable by imprisonment and death, we seized the opportunity when the French government opened its doors to us due to Grandpa's earlier involvement in the French Indochina era.

After the war, those who survived the genocide were strewn across the globe. Forever seeking asylum in foreign lands, the Hmong people have inherited perpetual oppression and persecution.

Above all things, life did not go back to normal for Father. Far and away from the land mines and the blood-soaked battlefields the fierce effects of the war remained deep in the soldier's soul. Many were believed to have succumbed to their traumas long ago. They survived the battlefields to die from deep within, a slow death caused by the effects of the war-related psychiatric disorders.

My father's situation was no different. The war left such detriment and horror that he sought refuge from the mental turbulences in total recluse. As most soldiers, if not all, he suffered from Post-Traumatic Stress Disorder (PTSD). Appropriate for that time, the disorder is often referred to as the post-Vietnam syndrome, a merciless mind-destroyer as some would call it.

At home, my family suffered the aftermath of his traumas. At first, we deluded ourselves into believing that it was just a passing phase, and that he would come back in all his debonair glory. But the evidence suggested otherwise and ultimately led us to accept that he would not likely recover from that apocalyptic epoch of his life. At times, he detached himself completely from his social duties including our family.

As my father became traumatized, his life turned from trite simplicity to delirium, a total dilapidation of the human spirit. His struggle with PTSD changed our father-son relationship for the worst. Not knowing better, I resented him for being absent in my life.

Inside his lonely mind, he was haunted by those whose lives he had taken in order to spare his own and by the soundtrack of rockets and shells hissing overhead that brought endless nightmares.

Men would always find any excuses for war, any excuses to test their weapons, any excuses to simply be men under the governance of a plethora of greed and *folie de grandeur*, he would always tell us. What is there to do against a culture that values war far more important, on account of profitability, than peace?

Nothing has changed today. Nor will it ever for that matter.

From the direct participation of such exhibition of evil, trauma and suffering were all that he found—his fall afterward.

Father had escaped death more times than he could recount, but one particular event stuck in his mind exceptionally, one that involved a bombardment at the Long Cheng military airbase that left him unconscious for three days. Long Cheng is also remembered as one of the busiest airports in the world during the Vietnam War.

He only narrated the event on a few occasions, when he was himself, but at each time it was with a somber tone interrupted with dreadful silences. Being brought back in those moments was a punishment just short of hell itself. Father shook his head ruefully whenever he made mention of the atrocities of war he'd witnessed, but it was therapeutic somehow, and since he rarely spoke in a lengthy way, we listened each time as if it were the first.

By my memory, it was a muggy day during midsummer before the fall of Long Cheng the following year. As always, the air was infested with mosquitoes. For some reason, that single detail had always been highlighted in the account. Perhaps, it brought a sense of normalcy to the gruesome nature of the story but I'd never asked him the reason. Sometimes a personal input is only relevant to the storyteller leaving it entirely to the audience to make their own interpretation.

It was one of those cases.

That afternoon, my father's battalion was ordered to reinforce the perimeter and to supply ammunitions and provisions to the outskirt hangars that spread along the landing strip. By the time they were done, the secured area looked impregnable as though to prevent simultaneously both invasion and escape.

The unusually quiet day drew suspicion of a surprise attack, but because another location nearby had been the target of heavy bombardments since the early morning, the possibility was dismissed quickly. The commander in charge of the base had sent most of the soldiers to the battleground to help stabilize the situation. Only a small number of soldiers remained behind to secure the base.

Deep into the afternoon when the sun started to beat most of the men into crawling out of their uniforms, everyone went to cool off under the dense vegetation on the south side of the base. Even the sentries from the surveillance posts assigned to survey any suspicious activities had joined the rest of the posse. "Why would anyone want to conquer a place like this?" the men often joked.

Father and ten of his battled-scarred men were the last ones outside the perimeter hauling the unused materials back to the military trucks. When finally work was done, they took a five-minute break to share refreshment. As usual, most of the topics of conversation were the kinds only apt to men in these circumstances—details voluntarily omitted here—as they all tried to forget about the unbearable humidity.

That afternoon, it almost felt like it was just another day in their lives, another day where children played on that same land that had become a cemetery of memories from halcyon days, another day traipsing in the rice fields or hunting in the jungle for deer and wild boar.

The war has depicted a different image since then.

In those days of zealotry, the landscape had lost much of its beauty, disfigured with huge craters made by years of bombing and deforestation to build military bases, roads and trenches—where once arable lands were now became battlefields. The only things that were still present and untouched were the mosquitoes. Both the war and Agent Orange had failed to rid of them.

Before my father could finish sipping the last drop of water from his gourd, a whirring in the sky broke the silence of the afternoon. A rocket-propelled grenade struck the truck in front of him into pieces. Rocks and dirt flew loose sending dust swirling about. The explosion shook the ground and sent him off fifteen feet in the air. Some men were heard shouting before a volley of gunfire ensued. Seconds later, another rocket blew up the truck he stood by earlier.

Three days later, he woke up in an infirmary bed under a huge military tent that also sheltered many more wounded soldiers. By the side of the bed, stood a nurse and one of his good friends.

He did not have much recollection of the incident.

All he remembered was the deafening sound of the first explosion followed by a blinding bright light before the sky caved in on him.

Beyond that point, all was darkness.

Miraculously, my father had no life-threatening wounds except for minor burns on his arms and back caused by shards of flying shrapnel. Halfway back to life, there was a buzz in his head. Something was not quite in place, a feeling he knew all too well. None of his men were inside the hospital tent.

His mind quickly filled with inquietudes.

In his bewilderment, he asked his friend about the whereabouts of his brothers-in-arms. No answer came from the teary-eyed man who kept looking at the tips of his muddy worn-out camouflage boots.

The silence spoke volumes.

Chapter 3

Bricks and Mortar

Caught in a flurry of silent panic from a glance at the steep ravine, the young woman held on tightly to the reins to keep the charcoal steed moving steadily forward. Following close behind, in tandem, two mules transported medical supplies and provisions. The drifting wind whistling through the gradient terrain and the narrowly winding mountainous pathway made the journey all the more difficult. A single misstep from the creatures and the fall would be fatal.

With her heart thrumming out of tune, she contracted cramps. In a desperate attempt to banish the queasy impulses, she focused on the road despite the pain that grew time and again insufferable. Still, a few kilometers of morning mist separated her from the in-the-clouds village destination.

In hindsight, she should have listened to her mother and remained home. But, encumbered with obligation she assumed the mission—a calling she couldn't ignore. Too many elderly people and ailing children stunted by malnutrition in those remote areas depended on the precious cargo.

The young woman contained her fear with jubilant thoughts about the growing new life inside of her. Alone, as were the Hmong women in her village, she carried on. The men, and all the boys tall enough to carry a riffle, have gone off to war to fight for a cause they neither sought nor understood. They were told that their sacrifices would allow their people to breathe freely again the air of their homeland and imbibe from the river streams that had sustained life there for many generations now, and many more to come. Reneged promises, history would reveal in the end, were all they received.

Taken by fear, she implored her ancestors for spiritual guidance and wished to return unharmed to her other children at home. The due date was approaching and impatience irked the fetus. She felt the seed of life moving, gamboling even, eager to come out of her womb.

Somewhere in this hostile territory while slipping into an abyss of solitude, she reveled in quiet merriment to calm her qualms.

The day I was born, as the story was told, my mother

was conducting a humanitarian exploit and barely made it home for delivery. She stands not very tall, even on her toes, but her unshaken will surpasses any obstacle that life presents to her. A larger-than-life woman, she is the indefatigable running engine and the thriving force of our family.

Throughout her life, Maman was embattled within her own illiteracy, a sorrowful affliction caused by her father, who pulled her out of the school system at a young age at the protests of all her teachers. Unfortunately, their efforts could not deter his determination. Grandpa, whose antediluvian beliefs defied the ages, had a different purpose for her, one that constituted being a good wife and raising healthy children. That single eventuality took the glimmer out of her eyes.

To this day, what's still eating at her remains her illiteracy.

When we arrived in France after the war officially ended, she faced the challenge of the language barrier. It wasn't long before she realized that she must carve a place for herself in this new world in order to survive. What really set her off came to light with an incident involving a distant relative who refused to help her with translation.

The woman scolded Maman for infringing upon her very freedom—freedom of being left alone, that is. She went as far as telling mother that we had no place in France and would be better off back to the old country.

To die was surely what she meant because death was all that was left there.

Maman did not say a thing and walked away.

Anyone suggesting that the incident left a dent of tragedy on her spirit and drowned her in desperation would've been dead wrong. On the contrary, this presented the first wake-up call in our early life in France. She found out the hard way that there was no hope to run to, only reality to face. But that's not entirely what drove my mother. I suspect what did was something of greater human decency, something called humility.

I remember the fire in her eyes that day after she had been ridiculed. There isn't any easy answer to a disappointment but a strong conviction of the will to remain strong, she kept telling us. She sat us down in the middle of the furniture-empty living room of our apartment and stared at us, one by one, then said, "My children, from this day forward we will not ask anyone for help anymore. We shall only rely on ourselves. I promise."

Maman prefers to brace truth rather than false-hope. To hold faith at bay, she reminds herself constantly that sometimes small disasters breathe life to greater accomplishments.

What still humbles me today is that she never showed the slightest resentment toward that woman, not even a single huff. Five years down the road, the tables turned in her favor. She loaned that woman a lump sum of money, without taking any interest, to thank her for the life lesson of being self-sufficient in the new world. Though the circumstances were not clear at the time, some speculated a method of passive coercion, others an act of genuine ethics. All I know is that Maman isn't the kind of woman who would look into other people's misery in order to feel better about hers. Whichever might've been the case, I am incapable of such humanism. After all, there are immoral situations that can bring a happy grin upon anyone's face.

In order to keep her faith strong, my mother always honored her preaching and the rewards came in forms of accomplishments. During the first nine months after the incident, she learned the basics of the French language in adult school before being released into the wilderness of the working world. Over time, the language barrier never stopped her from getting a job nor acquiring higher positions. With perseverance, she worked her way up to become the top quality controller at a denim jeans company while her weekends were devoted to generate more income to make ends meet.

Everyone who knew our family thought that she'd lost her mind when she got involved in the precious metal business. They had a valid point. She clearly lacked the education to understand the fluctuation of the stock market (La Bourse de Paris). In their minds, it was an act of defiance against logic. But Maman quickly proved everyone wrong. In surgical precision, her business acumen brought in fruitful revenues. She bought ingots of gold in times of Bear Market and turned them into bracelets, necklaces, and other accessories before selling them for a higher margin of profit in Bull Market. Considering that she was not part of a refined background and could barely write her name, that was impressive.

As life would have it, her success did not sit well with those whose emotions started to distill with jealousy. What can an illiterate woman with a sick husband and so many mouths to feed do? That mindset was part of the habitual mockery that spreads gossip faster than wild fire around us. To most people, we were at the bottom of the social ladder, and a promising future was simply out of reach.

In the end, it was none other than these people who directly contributed to Maman's success. And for that, I could not thank them enough.

Needless to say, her success also came with a price. Between her forever busy schedule and my father's post-traumatic condition, we were faced at early an age to care for each other. The majority of us were raised by the eldest of the siblings at best they could. On rare occasions when she was available and home, she would spend a few hours to tend to our individual needs.

Being in her company became an object of desire, almost a privilege. I was sad every day when my friends were picked up by their mothers after school. For years, I wore a joker-smile to hide the weight of reality so that my sadness would not affect my little brother.

Maman was always working, Father was always sick, so I was up for the job, no questions asked. No children should have to live through that kind of unfairness, but unfortunately not everyone is born a Rockefeller. Having grown up with what little we had, I learned to accept what was at hand and not to expect what might never come.

It was also expected that, soon or later, with all the responsibilities of the family on her shoulders, that she would become overbearing and more demanding in our discipline. She had no choice but to adopt the toughness of a drill sergeant. And so her stern ways fomented rebellion in some of us. For my part, I bargained with my brother V, the authority figure in her absence, for some extra TV time. In exchange for his silence, I would write love letters on his behalf to his many girlfriends. By the time I turned twelve, I had become a veritable pocket-Hugo.

To prepare us for the hardship of life, mother made sure that we received the best education possible. She believes education to be the stepping-stone to success, although with a variance: Education and Intelligence being two different animals. One is acquirable, the other is a gift that needs constant nurturing as to a new-born.

Regardless of the hardship, she never allows any of us to show any sign of weakness, a sure indication of defeat according to her beliefs. In one of her most profound analogies of life, she often reminded us that a good mind is all she gave us to slay the dragon, and not a sword. Shamefully, I did not fully grasp the concept until much later on, long after the foolish impulses of youth had ceased to control my life.

Or should I say, until now.

As much as there was success, there were also set-backs. The financial burden on her shoulders got heavier when one of my sisters moved to Paris to pursue an Haute Couture career. The tuitions, let alone her living expenses, were ridiculously costly. But Maman was not a bit intimidated. Instead, she rolled up her sleeves higher. All she ever wanted was for us to fully explore our potentials and have the life that she never had.

Beyond that point, we saw her even less.

Come what may, she would never part from her priorities. Her inner strength extended far beyond the ordinary, something that she had not bequeathed onto me in great quantity.

In that early stage of our lives, everything seemed to have deliberately conspired against us as we faced one challenge after another. Silhouetted by setbacks, our lives became a sad tale that carried hardships as installments to a never-ending debt.

No matter the circumstances, Maman always carried the weight of her responsibilities with appropriate gravitas. Nothing seemed strong enough to dampen her determination. To her credit, she had accomplished incredible exploits that even the most resolute of men would have only dreamed of achieving. For that matter, we've always compared her to the likes of other strong personalities such as Margaret Thatcher.

Today, I am grateful and proud to say that, had it not been for her unbreakable will, the spirit of our family would have been lost long ago, somewhere in the misty mountainous pathways of our lost homeland.

The woman of steel, indeed.

Chapter 4

Into the Furnace

Please, don't hit me anymore. I'm begging you."

"Shut up, or I'll kick you harder! And stop crying!"

"Please—no more! I'm hurt!"

"Didn't I tell you to shut up? Are you stupid or what?"

"Somebody, help me!"

"Ha, ha, ha! No one is here! Just you and me, chubby ugly kid."

"*Nooo*!"

Wham! Slamming of the door.

Soon after, I heard some heavy treads slowly stomping away. I was locked-up in the storage room. Pitch black. Dead silence.

I was suffocating in that hermetic tiny room. I expectorated wads of bloody phlegm and coughed convulsively. I pled and cried out for help, "Papa, where are you? Please save me!"

I was frightened. I felt the incipient anger rise. I felt its strength. I had mixed emotions. Fear took over my senses. I hated my life. I was in a state of doldrums, powerless and mostly alone—in my darkness.

The cavalry never arrived.

In conformity with undefiled family ethics and keen regard for tradition, my folks extended their hospitality to a young man for an undisclosed amount of time after he had lost his job and everything else to his name. According to my father, he was the son of a deceased fellow soldier from the old country.

That unwitting decision led to the most horrendous attempt at my humanity at the tender age of six. This was one of those moments that would define my life and my folks would live to regret it. But, then again, no one could have predicted, much less changed, the outcome, that far ahead.

The person I am about to describe has no characteristics of a common man, which is why I have no scruples in calling him the Minotaur.

At the cost of innocence lost, he served as the instrument to my dehumanization. The crimes he committed against me were of biblical proportion. Once I was in his destructive path, there was no turning back. My fate was sealed.

At the first sight of that young man, I sensed a devilish set-aflame aura surrounding him. A hunch. There was an element of suspicion about that man that drew my attention immediately—his unfriendly demeanor.

From that first meeting, I was most perplexed by the constant glare of anger in his eyes that showed the same expression as if tattooed on his face. That fierce look had never failed to make the hairs on the back of my neck tingle.

It wasn't long until my premonition came to full fruition.

The first assault occurred when I was left under his supervision one Monday morning that I had been kept home with a case of the flu. At his convenience, the desolate environment presented the perfect crime scene, and he seized the opportunity to unleash his fury upon me. As soon as everyone left, he lured me into the storage room with a Kinder chocolate egg and secured tightly the door behind.

As a predator in ambush mode, he first observed me with patience while I gorged myself with the egg to uncover the toy inside. His eyes hinted at violence but without facts, instinct is anything but mere assumption. I did not know better. I was just a kid. Then without warning, instant fear.

I remember the strength of his arms as he yanked me close to him.

Throngs of menacing looks drilled through my eyes.

The silence was broken when he smacked my head so violently it seemed uprooted from my neck. I squealed in protest from the pain as he knocked the wind out of me. My heart quickened from fear.

A sense of trust betrayed.

In that moment of horror, a wrench of lucidity brought awareness into his eyes, an apparent expression of nervousness. He remained unrepentant nonetheless. No guilt. He realized that the punishment needed moderation to avoid any bruising. With one arm, he scooped me swimmingly like a rag doll from the floor and shook me awake.

While seeking for my cognitive functions, I focused on the faint light coming through a small crack on the door to avoid being consumed by the pain.

His bestiality had deceived me to believe that he was made of something primitive, intelligence-deprived. A big mistake on my part.

By the time I regained full consciousness, I could almost see a grain of fear in his eyes. Trying to suppress the rising panic, I probed his face for any sign of humanity. Just in case. Incredibly, there was nothing remotely of that nature in it that would qualify as such. I was at the center of the storm.

His hands clenched into fists, and the look in his eyes

quickly changed back to the anger mode as if customary.

A glutton for sadism, the savage showed no signs of mortification to have caused offense. The treatment I received that day was beneath contempt.

The Minotaur remained irredeemable.

Aside from the cussing, he spoke only a few civilized words to insist that it was necessary a preparation to man me up, as he put it. His notion of teaching, he claimed. But the evidence of violence pointed to a different motive. Clamping both hands on my temples, he instructed me repeatedly not to cry. Then he slapped me again, but this time with less intensity that left disappearing imprints of his paw*s* across my burning rouge cheeks.

The hyena sardonic-grin was all I remembered at that moment.

At such times, the last thing on my mind was to provoke more punishments hoping he'd stop the onslaught, although I did not put much stock on that possibility. Something was telling me that I was not out of the woods. I found myself in a situation where evil dictated everything to the modicum of detail.

For a short while, I felt a secret resistance rise but I refrained from voicing out loud my rebellion, to which the Monster would not approve. By engaging his demonic instincts, I knew that all I would achieve would only aggravate the Minotaur to more violence toward me.

The fight was over before it even started. A slip of the tongue would mean the end, futile suicide by idiocy.

Paralyzed like a frightened mouse, I could not even make a run for it to escape his tentacles. I must soldier on with the pain, was all I was thinking.

By some miracle, two hours after the assault initially began he decided I had my fair share of torture for the day and stopped cold. He was probably exhausted from punishing me, I thought. But, neither was I feeling relieved nor in any way safe. After a short trip to the kitchen, he brought back some ice cubes wrapped in a hand towel and pressed the moist ensemble against the right side of my head to reverse the swelling. I did not put out a single groan from the cold, straining for insight of what might've caused that man to lose all aspects of his humanity.

One thing was sure. The Minotaur lived well below moral principles and consciously embraced his animalistic side. He was evil before he was anything else. And perhaps, that was just that.

After that first incident, a series of events happened frequently as he gained more confidence. I had initially thought that this sort of devilry required experience, but he later admitted that I was his first and only real victim. A personal milestone judging by the smirk on his face that revealed a rack of tar-stained yellow teeth. Supposedly, neither time nor the proper location had allowed him to prepare the other potential victims for manhood. All he managed with them amounted to no more than a pinch. The lucky ones, I thought with an inward sigh.

In crisp definition, I still remember all the punishments and the psychological scars that would never properly heal. And most of all, the dark storage room that served as a Gulag torture chamber. He kicked me, pinched me, bit me, slapped me, and beat me down like an animal. He took heinous pleasures in each and every blow and called me a worthless chubby ugly little kid. For some reason, the verbal abuse seemed to have more impact on me than the physical violence.

Enough was never enough with that man. He threatened me with more violence in order to keep our ordeal out of anyone's suspicion. I wouldn't dare say a word or even think it. What choice did I have? I was just a kid.

Every other day, the infliction of torture occurred in variation of methods and in numbers. Just like his mood swings, they were unpredictable. As the carnage went on, the thrill of torturing me made my existence nothing more than a contribution to his entertainment.

As the days turned into weeks, he forced me to hold my arms in a crucifixion pose for a long period of time. When I lowered them from fatigue, he struck me on the shoulder blades with a wide wooden ruler. By then, he had accumulated a vast knowledge in the torture department and made me wear a jacket to absorb most of the punishment.

If he could have, he would have tortured me to death.

To think otherwise never crossed my mind.

At the height of his power over me, the abuse escalated far above the germinal phase. He used thinner bamboo sticks to hit the tips of my fingers and made me kneel down on rough surfaces until my knees became numb. The objective was the same, endurance while keeping a straight face.

After a few more one-to-one sessions, he introduced me to pornography. As might be expected, molestation was also part of the demonic ritual. He would order me to pull down my pants and touch me inappropriately. The early afternoons after school were usually our alone porn-popcorn-time. In each occasion, he would masturbate in front of me. I didn't have the slightest clue of what he was doing and just stared at him feeling uneasy.

To no one's surprise, he was without a woman. During his stay not a single damsel came along, and even those in distress refused his help. It's only understandable since he wasn't exactly the Brad Pitt of the day. But to be fair, it was his unfriendly demeanor that shriveled off the enthusiasm of any potential mate.

Or perhaps, one might argue, that the big winner was his rancid breath, which might've also explained why I lost my appetite for a while. The odor of his decaying teeth and his rotten gums was nothing short of nauseous. It had that distinctive garlicky and raw sewage stench to it—a lit matchstick could have possibly ignited a dragon jet fire out of his gullet.

The Minotaur made sure that his dominance was omnipresent. A devoted voyeur, he often stalked me at school during recess time. Even at the dinner table, the intimidation went on with the same ruthless efficiency. The smell of fear was all over me but no one took notice of it.

My soul was crying for liberation but I knew that he would hurt me if I were to tell anyone. He'd whisper the same dreaded words to my ears over and again, premeditated to engage my innermost primal sense, fear. "Tell anyone, and I will finish you off. If you think that you got it bad, you're in for a big surprise. I can easily hurt your family as well, so think about it, you worthless chubby ugly little kid. You think hard about it."

Above all, it was his eyes that made me tremble in fear. Those rolling angry eyes had left me more times than I can recall feeling bruised a full slap across the face could have never managed. For the longest time, I could not be left alone in the presence of any male adults without shaking to my core.

In desperation, I went in great lengths in trying to win his affection. Without success, however. I couldn't locate his reason because there was none. And yet I refused to abandon hope. I was persuaded that by uncovering his God-given side the violence would cease. But such a possibility, too small to even consider, remained a distant dream nowhere to materialize in the foreseeable future.

From time to time, when he'd let his guard down I could sense the little kid inside him. That kid was probably my age which made me understand why he chose me. A reflection of him, I was the cast away, rejected from the rest of the posse and mostly alone, the perfect prey. In fact, if we shared anything in common it was only our loneliness.

More battered inside than outside, I wet my bed long after he was gone. From that period of time forward, I lived in fear and developed disdainful feelings toward the outside world.

I hated my life.

To this day, my parents know only little of that unspoken truth. I have spared them the grisly details. Sometimes things are best kept secret. Or perhaps, those experiences still dwell with embarrassment and discomfort in my soul.

Long after his departure, I was told that the Minotaur, at the age of seven, lost all his family members before his eyes in a fatal ambush during the Vietnam War. He escaped to Thailand on his own with the help of other war orphans. It was said that he swam across the Mekong River to the Thai border where he was administered to a refugee camp. Word spread that he was brutally beaten and sexually assaulted there by the guards on a daily basis.

At first, the news of his past brought me quiet satisfaction, but before long I realized the consolation as immoral and cruel.

He was just another victim of dire circumstances,

broken by events he could neither control nor escape.

Today, I understand that he had punished me all those months to avenge himself.

News came a few years later that he was serving time in a maximum security prison on battery and rape as a result of sodomy charges of a young boy. The deeds he couldn't confess came back to haunt him after all. As part of the culture inside the Big House, the condition of living for a *chomo* was the least favorable one, and quickly he became a commodity among inmates. This time, he was a victim of his own crimes.

His trauma had become something incurable, a permanent darkness. The kind no one comes back from.

No matter the amount of comfort, my early life had been caucused by the passage of violence at his hands. Nothing would ever be the same anymore. For the longest time, I lived in fear and sought refuge within my inner sanctuary, the comfort zone, the only place where I found safety and protection from the evil of men.

The emptiness grew steadily inside while the anger slowly brewed, anger mostly aimed toward myself for being so weak, one step away from ebullition.

My soul had been stained.

Chapter 5

Dethroned

Autumn finally manifested its first tantrums, and along came the rain. In an instant, the murky sky chased away the tranquility of the morning while the rousing winds dispersed the withered sycamore leaves all over our sleeping *faubourg*. Off on the horizon, the presumptuous storm announced its arrival with a display of lightning bolts. Boisterous as a band of medieval troubadours, the elements took center stage and painted a mind-gobbling tableau of their legendary fury that would have marveled any fastidious masters of the brush.

From the edge of a wide open window I stared out at the rain and let it revive my soul. Only the wind-driven tumbleweeds from those famous Clint Eastwood's Westerns were missing in this scenario. In a stand-still, I was lost in thoughts. A mirthful sentiment came over me.

I became as one with the rain.

Moments later, a little voice disrupted the whirl of fracas inside my head and delivered me from delirium. The voice, almost inaudible, was muffled by the endless resounding of the thunder that became louder by the second. Halfway detached from reality, I glanced over my shoulder and scoped out my little brother camouflaged underneath a color-faded purplish duvet.

Despite the fact that he was many years my junior, we were inseparable. Throughout our childhood, I made sure that all his caprices were met with diligence.

Quivering relentlessly, the little one was frightened by the thudding ruckus and the deluge of drips pelting against the exterior walls of our bedroom that seemed, for an instant, made out of friable layers of papier-mâché. As always, he was terrified of the discontentment of the storm and I, absorbed in thoughts, nearly forgot about his fragile emotions. I flashed a smile to bring contrast to his weariness and pinched his rouged cheeks. After clearing my throat, I lulled his anguish in the safety of my arms to reassure him of my devotion apropos his well-being.

In synchrony with the slowing of the wind, his cries turned into silence. When finally the sound of the elements died down, I heard the gurgling noise of hunger raging from his bowels. I tossed him on my back as I often had when he was a toddler and headed toward the kitchen. Because it was still early in the morning, our sanctuary was empty of any awakened soul, no yawning to be heard for at least another couple of hours. Without further delay, I fixed an omelet with toasted garlic bread, and we indulged breakfast as two hungry cubs coming out of hibernation.

The rain poured still.

I am the penultimate child of a nest of far-too-many siblings. At one time, I was rumored to be the last one until another fellow came along, accidentally and dethroned my rightful emplacement in the family hierarchy. "Perhaps your folks did not own a TV back in the day," people would often tease me. I never found much humor in that. In reality, I was internally affected by the birth of my little brother. His arrival shook off my world as he unintentionally stole the spotlight. Much to my displeasure, my mother spent less time with me to tend to the more urgent needs of the new born. Unable to understand the situation, I felt abandoned, in desperate need of attention.

Despite the shrubbery of secretive jealousy that outlined our brotherhood, there was no apparent feeling of resentment on my end, at least not at the conscious level. As the years went on, I kept on providing that extra care and love for him, hoping that our mother would spare me a scrap of affection in return.

For what little it might be worth, it was in fact the episode with the Minotaur that brought us even closer as it ossified my responsibility to protect him at all cost. Although I must admit one incident at the playground did escape my vigilance.

The whole thing could've been avoided had I not been preoccupied catcalling. What can I say? I had an early start in that field. In that short amount of time of distraction, he got himself in some major entanglement. A set of gypsy twins felt cheated when they lost all their glass marbles to him and pushed him off the slider out of poor sportsmanship. He fell face-down on the sandy ground and hurt himself badly. The whole incident happened so fast that it took me a few seconds to compute everything.

My little brother wouldn't hurt a fly, even if his life depended on it.

Instantaneously, the tambour of warfare played out loud in my head. As I approached the twins to investigate the incident, their father put his hands up to stop my advancement. The mastodon saw the conviction in my eyes and understood that no investigation was to be conducted. I was out to exact revenge and collect their skulls as trophies.

The man threatened to make a big crêpe out of me if I did not clear the premises at once. All the while keeping my composure, I complied without resistance. I was no match for that big hairy man.

It was one of those situations where retreat was necessary in order to minimize the losses and injuries. But in the dark corner of my mind, I wasn't anywhere close to letting go of the incident.

We hardly made ten yards when the mother, a massive woman whose weight surpassed mine by about half, grabbed me by the right arm and slapped me twice before shoving me to the ground. Spitting saliva while mutilating her words, she yelled at my face in a dialect unknown even to the tongues of Babel. I assumed it was about her cross-eyed little angels.

A crowd gathered, watching in shock, flushed with blank faces, but none dared to intervene, something deeply alien to my upbringing. Was it de rigueur now to deny help to a fallen comrade? I asked myself, startled. This lack of communal commitment was disheartening. Any chance to get a phone number just fell through.

If I had failed in any endeavor requiring social interaction afterward, this event was to be blamed in major part. What I witnessed that day both educated and horrified me.

Still on the ground, I shouted to my little brother to run home. He did so without my telling him twice.

The husband grinned from ear to ear but a frosty glance from her made his face go straight again. For an instant of unspoken complicity, we came to a secretive man-to-man accord. She was an otherworldly scary-looking woman with deep dark skin, big intense eyes, and that D'Artagnan pencil mustache. Impressive.

She seemed to reproach him for not beating on me

himself. The coward did not say a word and just looked down. In a different set of circumstances, that would have been comical, but in this one, I remained silent, unable to recover from the buzzing in my ears.

Then rage.

It was high-noon. The heat was intense. The salty sweat stung my eyes. I was driven to the edge of madness. That was a characteristic I never before displayed to this level.

There was no need to think anymore, no need for pardon, no need for decency, no need to be civilized. Just a need to unleash—just unleash. Before I knew it, I punched her as hard as I could right above the urinary bladder. I felt the ring of lard around my fist jiggle on impact. She crouched in pain and screamed, "Oh no, you didn't—"

On my feet again, I did not wait around to hear the end of the sentence and fled like a thief in the night. The man took after me but quickly abandoned his odyssey to catch me when his tongue touched his chin after only a few steps.

Summer vacation was ruined. We had to stay away from our favorite playground to cool things off. We seldom mentioned it to anyone, although we retained the good humor from it, and we would deny the whole ordeal when asked.

Come fall, we took a different route to school to avoid any possible ambush. Those were the times that made me realize that life was necessarily tough to mold me into character. Years later in my late teens, I bumped into that family again at the local flea market. By then, I was not scared of them anymore. The roles were reversed.

As I reflect on those moments now, as small or insignificant as they may be, I understand that not only was I the big brother to the little guy but also the father figure we never had.

The emptiness widened.

Chapter 6

The Glory Beneath Her Wings

From the vantage point where I was standing, the scene was reminiscent of the premiere of a major play. The room filled quickly with an agitated mob from all ages. In front, the little ones sat in mixed-gender pairs on the floor, and everybody else was scattered behind in no particular order as in an amphitheater setting.

All lights were out while the throb of impatience grew in murmuring peeves as the show delayed.

The curtains, a set of beige chiffons, finally spread apart to the retribution of the spectacle-craving audience. Soon after, a fairly tall platinum-haired woman appeared wearing fancy color-matching clothes from head-to-toe.

Her presence immediately changed the atmosphere in the room.

Behind her proud upright posture, two unscented pillar candles lit up the little space she occupied. The rest of the room was obscure with ghostly movements on the walls. The shimmering of her sequined dress and mostly her revered presence brought everyone at awe. She received a warm standing ovation.

When she spoke her first words, everyone clung to each other without making a sound. As always, her eloquence captivated everyone's attention.

The show began.

Grandma's presence had always been a source of joy to us all. Eager to spend time in her much-appreciated company we could hardly wait for her next visit. A combination of warmth and tenderness, her language only contained terms of endearment. At one time or another, we all found comfort within her heartwarming embrace.

When she visited, the whole family and anyone else of privilege gathered to listen to her fables and folk tales for she was renowned for being a great story-teller. By a large margin, our favorite ones were macabre ghost stories. During her scariest bone-chilling narrations even the adults found themselves intertwined.

A sophisticated creature by nature, Grandma was outlandishly classy and always well-dressed as if every day was the first day of worship. In seeming contrast with my maternal grandma, *mémé*, she believed in living life to the fullest rather than soiling her hands with gardening and household chores.

Throughout my childhood, she had been a prominent figure of a unique genre. More often than I can recall, she had stood against my mother's harsh discipline about our education. The only problem was that she lived an hour away, so help did not always come in on time.

Despite all this, everything I've come to know about her changed in the space of a breath one morning. What I learned that day contributed to great pain and caused a seism shift in our relationship.

The poignant revelation came during a colorful argument with my brother H, whose words have always been a pervading harshness that ultimately turned physical. If ad hominem attacks had been what counted, H's undisputable ability in that field would have won him a Nobel Prize.

Things got quickly out of hand when I bit his left arm in self-defense and locked my jaws until he squealed like a piglet. In the heat of the moment, while rubbing off the deep marks left by my incisors, he uttered out of frustration, "No wonder nobody likes you! You take everything so seriously."

"Whatever *charogne*! You started the fight, so take that!" I replied.

"You maggot, I'm gonna squash you!"

"Forget you!" I screamed back at him.

Then out of nowhere, he started to laugh.

"What's so funny, Neanderthal?" I asked, puzzled.

"You're so ugly that even Grandma doesn't like you," he said, falling on his back from laughter.

"Whatever, *couillon*!"

"Ask anyone if you don't believe me. They'll tell you," he replied with a grin.

"Liar! She loves everyone the same way."

"Yea—everyone, except for you, fat ugly little thing," he added.

"Just shut your face!" By now my voice had quieted down considerably.

"You still don't believe me?" he asked in that sarcastic tone and then added, "When you were a baby, you were so ugly that she didn't even want to babysit you. Nobody wanted you, if you ask me." Laughter, again, plenty more that filled the silence in the room.

"Liar," I shouted. "Grandma is not like that!"

"We all know that she has always favored Thomas over you," he replied with a serious air.

Thomas was my first cousin, and we were about the same age, so the story started to hold some truth.

"When you guys were toddlers, she'd always leave you drenched in dirty diapers." He laughed again.

I didn't say anything else at that point.

"She neglected you 'cause you're so damn ugly," he added.

Lips tightened, I just listened.

"She only took care of Thomas, and one time you

were so hungry you ate your own feces." He laughed even harder upon those words.

"Grandma loves none more, none less!" I yelled out.

"You should check your facts, Fatso."

I got up and rushed in his direction, screaming and crying. He finally pinned me against the bed and put one knee on my back to hold me down.

"I'll let you go if you stop fighting and moving," he said.

But I refused to surrender.

"Stop, or else!"

Then our older brother walked in the room to separate us. We were punished and spent the rest of the day cleaning and running errands.

Unyielding at first, I wanted to believe that the whole story was made up, but somehow I'd come to terms with the fact that this had the prints of something larger. After dinner, my sister corroborated H's account of the incident and quashed all hope that might cast doubt on that reality.

It was a terrible blow. I was torn in anguish. I grew up under Grandma's care and never imagined that she would show favoritism toward anyone. Once again, I felt rejected by my own family. The truth produced a wreckage of emotional debris and left me in despondency.

Enervated by the news, I buried myself deeper in the catacombs of despair. It was only a matter of time before everything fell apart.

All the loving memories of her were gone as I was

incapable of steering my thoughts away from the inner turmoil. Being one of those who could not easily shrug off crisis without concern, I could find nothing to comfort me.

In the time since, when all the other kids in the family rushed to greet her, I was nowhere to be found. My love for her was morally bankrupt. I kept my distance and regarded her with a different eye. The sound of her voice became less soothing, her eyes less sincere, and her embrace turned cold. I tried to reconcile my feelings, but I could not run far enough from the truth.

Sensing that our relationship has been circling the drain, Grandma asked me one day to join her for a promenade. In small steps, we trailed to a nearby park, a once-serene place despoiled now by gentrification and infested with lovers who relished in feverish rendezvous.

As if to bring some sort of balance to the nocturnal activities, the Bellefontaine Park was always deserted in the morning, which gifted nature's lovers an intimate moment to rekindle with their inner peace. Aside from the persistent caws of a lone crow hopelessly seeking companionship, I assumed, the other birds barely made their presence notice.

Carefully, so as to not outpace her, I held her speckled hand as she walked slowly by me. On either side of the pathway, dense tall grass and seed-dispersed dandelions seemed to welcome us. When finally the walk had worn her down, we settled on an old color-chipped wooden bench by the algae-overrun pond. In the distance, young ducklings were dipping their beaks in and out of the water in search of small fish.

Busy observing their morning rituals, I had not noticed the glimmer in her eyes until I felt her tight grip on my hand.

She spoke suddenly, her voice clearly shaken, "My little one, I heard a disturbing story, and I wanted to clarify a few things with you."

"What is it, Granny?" I asked, although the answer was evident in her eyes.

"It was brought to my attention that I had shown favoritism between you and Thomas, and I wanted you to know the truth." She paused.

I wiped her tears away from her face with my thumbs. I knew exactly of which incident she was referring to but kept silent and just observed her effort at an explanation without interfering.

"I want you to know that the reasons were different," she added, choking up, "contrary to what you've been told." Another pause before she continued. "Unlike you, Thomas had always been a weak baby. And because I was concerned about his fragility, I had neglected you at times to tend more to him." After a sigh, she went on without trying to embellish the truth as she languished within her own guilt. "The incident that was brought to your attention did really happen. I am truly sorry."

Temporarily at a loss for words, she dried her tears

and then spoke again, "Know that I'm not proud of it and—"

I interrupted her, not wanting for her to undergo the torture further with more exhumations of painful memories.

Against the glint of the dew and the reflection of the morning sunshine on the surface of the water, I held both of her beautiful wrinkled pale hands to give her warmth from the gentle breeze of fall. With no real cause to effect a misery, I reassured her that all that mattered was the love that we shared at that very moment. That day, we both felt a sense of peace settle in.

The ducklings kept on feeding.

Chapter 7

The Olympian

It began as an ordinary morning, another morning staring out to the world as a birdcage perched between dreams far away from the madness within. Perhaps tomorrow would be a better day, I told myself without conviction.

That's what my life had come to. Anything good only happened in supposition. Anything bad, a reality. And worse, everything was handed to me without the availability of choice. My attempts at happiness proved to be unavailing, symptomatic of a curse.

Early that morning, Uncle K, my father's younger brother, came knocking on our door. I was no stranger to those steady and hard knocks, so I knew who it was. The only person up with me was my brother, Hercules, as I called him. He was the one before me and also the worst brother anyone could have landed.

A moment before Uncle K's arrival, we were having breakfast, *Pain Perdue* and two slices of a leftover homemade *Tarte-Au-Pommes*. Concocting breakfast was not a talent of mine, but that morning Hercules made it my field of expertise by indentured servitude. If not, my scalp was to be knifed off. As a mean of retaliation, I used the week-long expired milk for the *Pain Perdue*. Too busy abusing me in any way possible, he had neither noticed the surreptitious contentment in my eyes nor that I ate only the slice of pie.

Upon the fifth knock, I answered the door and stood there invisible as Uncle K inched past me without saying a word. He walked with haste to Hercules, a few gift bags under his arms. In rhapsodic admiration, he tapped him on the shoulder and said, "Congratulations, buddy! I heard that you have terrific grades this trimester."

Before the last word was entirely pronounced, he pulled two delicately wrapped presents out of the bags and handed both to my brother, who accepted them with delighted eyes. Hercules tore up the wrappers with mythical strength and uncovered a huge scientific calculator and some Japanese action figures, the pioneers of what would be the Power Rangers of today.

There was nothing else in the bags. Nothing else to my name. Insulted, I took a short trip to hell from jealousy, but kept my *sangfroid.* The empty living room reflected on the void inside, and with breakfast stuck in my throat, I felt out of place.

Perhaps, I was being tested. I suggested to myself.

But that was unlikely the case here. Hercules was everything I was not. In my next life, I would come back as him. I set my plate aside.

"Hercules, *Le Magnifique*," I said quietly to myself with an overly-exaggerated southern accent. Disappointed and mostly hurt, I indulged myself with a little note of sarcasm. I was entitled to that much, I thought. At least that.

After a while, Uncle K's glance strayed in my direction, and finally he acknowledged my presence. He gave me a fictitious smile, the kind that would bury anyone deeper in self-pity. He spoke not a single word still and turned his attention back to Hercules. I was revolted at how a man of his stature, at least in my eyes, could act so repulsively.

While they were conversing, I filled the blank in my soul by watching the morning cartoon programs. I must have watched the entire "Tom & Jerry" saga that morning. *How many times that stupid cat is going to swallow and spit out that adrenaline-supercharged little mouse?* I thought, pulling a reluctant smile and annoyed by their indifference. So desperate was I to be included in their discussion that I would have been satisfied with a simple greeting.

A claustrophobic environment closed in quickly.

After an infinite moment of gratification, Uncle K finally got up and told my brother again, "Congratulations and keep it up, buddy!" Then he sprang on his feet to meet my father, who had just come out of his bedroom feeling groggy.

"Man, this kid is such a regenerative force! He's gonna make something out of himself someday, just you watch!"

"I hope so! I surely wish for all of them to have a good life," my father replied softly.

The atmosphere quickly became awkward. By the look of it, it seemed that my uncle was more proud and excited about my brother's achievements than my father was.

But that was not the case. Father was a taciturn man who preferred to pursue life in simplicity under the shadow of humility. He believed that the opinion of the outside world should not be of any astute relevance to personal fulfillment. He'd always emphasized that keeping one's head above the clouds was probably the hardest thing to do in life. Father was also the oldest among his brothers, and other than for that fact they looked up to him for his wisdom as well.

"Let's make sure that Einstein here becomes a renowned brain surgeon or a rocket scientist even!" Uncle K added.

My father just nodded approval and looked in my direction. For some reason, he did not come to my rescue.

Their insensitive exchange gave me the feeling that I was the only one committed to the ideal of equality and respect in the family anymore. Indignant, I cleaned my plate, and without stomping on the floor, which would have been absolutely forgivable considering the situation, I dismissed myself quietly.

What an injustice! I too have good grades. Why didn't I get any rewards for my efforts? I thought angrily. I went back to my bedroom window to observe the clouds for any chance of a Fata Morgana to appear in the horizon. That morning, harmony was fractured once more.

I initially intended a different life.

An outcast, even at home, I lived incognito in spiritual seclusion. Come to think of it, I had never taken any family pictures. When I was growing up, only a handful of people knew that I was part of the family.

As hard as it was to deal with one sibling stealing the spotlight, I also suffered favoritism from another. In some ways, I was grateful that life had conditioned me to brace against any disappointments early enough. It did not make me necessarily stronger but more accepting of what I could not change.

Hercules inherited his tall genes from my father's side, and he never let me forget. Over the years, the size disproportion between us grew even greater, which became a source of considerable discomfort for me.

While I stood not much higher above the ground, he

was the tower of the family. As if the humiliation was not enough, he had one of those distinctive Greek noses that really accentuated his appearance.

To the family and relatives, he belonged to a different order and lifted their pride to places I could only dream of existing. I would have settled being a particle of dust in that universe.

For consolation, Maman always reminded me of my unique attribution, *the gift of goodness* as she put it. She explained further that nature has a certain way to compensate where one lacks.

Her words did not make me feel better.

My misery became Hercules's substance abuse. There wasn't a single day that went by without us fighting and me crying afterward. These constituted the real reasons that made me resent him for most of my life.

If memory serves, we had not had much meaningful moments as brothers—I could actually make a count. To this day, I'm not quite sure what possessed him, out of concern, it seemed, and seemingly out of character at the same time, to ask me this question during a time in which he suffered a broken ankle and I had to care for him: "Why do you always distance yourself from all of us?"

To which I answered enigmatically, "You would not understand. It can be quite challenging to be me." Little did he know that so many times I had wished to crawl under his skin just to see the beauty of a normal life through his lens.

Clueless and unpolished in his manners, he asked another question. "Why are you only happy when it rains?"

I knew that an honest answer would only invite more questions, and I had not wished to continue with the interrogation. Also, that part of me I did not want to share with anyone, much less with him. So I simply replied, "Because a spotless blue sky is a lonely sky."

When it rains, Maman always stays home.

Chapter 8

The Road

Lost in a chimerical abandon, I drifted high among the bluish clouds. Within a quick turn of the weather, I felt few drops of rain gliding off of my face before splashing against the century-old cobblestone pavement. The drops increased in greater frequency for a moment but stopped suddenly despite the saturated clouds above that threatened a downpour.

Pensively, I heard a distant voice in the back of my mind, murmuring my name in quick repetition. I turned to identify the person who had just pulverized that moment of peace and I found my French teacher, Madame Verdure, standing next to my fifteen kg backpack a few yards away.

She held in her hand the revolting beanie that my mother had packed earlier that morning. I refused to wear it because my friends had remarked that it resembled a wimple worn by deacon nuns. I hid the embarrassment under a frigid mask of pretentious coolness to slough off my discomfort.

Madame Verdure approached to hand over my belongings. "You need to wear this," she said, lifting the dreaded beanie. The endearment in the tone of her voice was surprisingly tender and expressive of a motherly concern. It was the first time that I'd seen, or anyone else for that matter, that unrevealed velvety side of hers. No one would believe me if I attempted to tell a soul, I thought.

"Okay," I lied.

In a scowling expression, she gave me another concerned look. "Is anyone coming for you?"

It was about forty-five minutes after the bell had rung, and everyone else except the groundskeeper had cleared the school premises by then. Standing on top of a gopher hole, a garden hose in his hand and a grimace on his face, the old man was trying to flush out the creatures.

"*Sapristi,* be gone already or drown!"

With a hasty glance, I redirected my attention back at Madame Verdure. "Yes. Someone has surely been dispatched for me."

We exchanged smiles, and for one frightening moment I thought she would never leave. I just wanted to return to my soliloquy trance while awaiting impatiently for the arrival of the rain.

It never came that day, not a single mutter of thunder. I kept my words unspoken in silent rebellion.

She understood and left.

The clouds parted.

I was alone.

By the time Madame Verdure was out of sight, I had resettled nearby a willow tree intrigued by a drone of beetles flying in disaccord in search of a refuge from the howling wind. A moment later, my sister Song arrived and led me to a constricted road that we often took as a short-cut back to the neighborhood. On we went, along the serpentine pathway that pervaded through a botanical garden and a vast elongated area of greenery situated in the middle of the menacing tall buildings. For obvious resemblance, the scenery had an intimate touch of Central Park, though at a much smaller scale.

As we walked under the dormant maple trees, we were ambushed by dead leaves tossing and swirling about in all directions. In an instant, the cold air seized me. My thin parka could not shield me against the impetuous mistrals.

Halfway through the trail, I noticed my sister's impassive expression. She was known to be free-spirited and of good humor, but that day she was nearly a morsel of herself. With sightless eyes, she had not said a word the entire time.

Wise beyond my years, I kept to myself for the rest of the walk.

Once we reached the parking lot of our apartment building, I saw Uncle K drive off. He seemed preoccupied and did not notice our presence. He rarely visited anymore having moved to a different town, and when he did, it was usually during the weekends. I glanced at my sister from the corner of my eyes for an explanation.

No answer.

We entered the warm apartment and walked into the living room. The rest of the siblings were already there except for the little one who had choir rehearsal until six o'clock. They were mumbling in whispers. Most of them should have not been even home yet, and that doubled my fear of a tragedy.

In a panicked voice, I asked Hercules to debrief me. The heartless beast placed his hand over my mouth to hush me and ignored my plea completely. His attitude only sparked more curiosity, but no one helped spirit away my worries.

The room had been quiet for a minute when all of a sudden the phone rang, and within three rings of terror my brother V answered the call. Numb with stupor, I felt a creepy sentiment galvanize our worst fear into mass hysteria.

Uneasy, I approached to listen to the conversation when Song grabbed my arm and held me back, stifling a sob. V pulled the telephone cord and disappeared into the kitchen. The dreadful silence only intensified the suspense. I suspected the worst to have happened, as the case might be.

After a petrifying motionless moment, V finally came out and spoke up in a hesitant voice. "Father has had an accident at the metallurgic plant," he said. "He was taken to the ER, where Maman has been with him since the early morning. After the first diagnosis, it is not clear if he will ever walk again."

The silence was interrupted by a room filled with lachrymose souls as we grappled with relentless despair. Everyone clung to each other in prayers. Despite our young ages, we understood the gravity of the situation. On a positive note, the event had brought all of us closer for the first time.

Father remained at the hospital more than a couple of weeks, and we took turns visiting him before he was transferred to Geneva to be treated for sciatica by specialists. Due to the constraints imposed by distance, only our mother traveled back and forth to see him mostly on the weekends.

Twelve long months passed before he was finally released from the hospital. The injuries he sustained healed considerably well and were not as severe as initially diagnosed. But the miracle had not come without a price. He would not be able to work again.

In the immediate aftermath of the accident, the family's financial situation became even more precarious. As money was scarce, our mother only prioritized our basic needs. To compensate for the financial crisis that we faced, she signed me up, along with Hercules, to a summer program with the local Catholic Church that sent off less-fortunate children to stay with host families.

The novelty of the experience shook me to the core. I begged her not to send me away but she insisted that it would be to my benefit to learn more about the French culture and to expand my horizon.

Father was diametrically opposed to the idea, but she did what she thought was best for all of us. Her decision was conceived out of necessity.

A part of me had wished to tell her about the ordeal I just went through at the hands of the Minotaur, but I kept silent. The timing was not favorable. My problems were no more than background noises compared to the arising hardship that threatened our family life.

Any chance at recovery would have to wait.

At the train station, I stared at Maman as though it would be my last time in her company. We were just a few feet away but it seemed as if we were worlds apart. The paleness of her face from endless sleepless nights worried me. More than anyone else, she deserved to be happy.

This unfortunate situation allowed me to put my own sentience of the reality into perspective and to take a different approach toward life. I willfully surrendered my recovery for her well-being. I never had any cause to regret it. She was the only pillar in a world that was crumbling apart.

Upon arrival to our destination, I was immediately separated from Hercules. It was a different France inside the France that I knew, far away from the projects of the gray cement city that was home.

Ahead of resettlement, it was common practice for refugee parents to give away their children for adoption for a chance at a better life. And although the odds were improbable, I prayed that was not the case.

The void inside me widened to the size of Vy Canis Majoris.

Chapter 9

Spiritually Unavailable

Tumbling down and getting up just as quickly, I zigzagged through a group of pupils with an eruption of sweat overflowing the periphery of my forehead. At that frightening moment, I felt as if I had grown wings.

At breath's end, I came face-to-face with a dead end, a long wall. I attempted to leap over but came up short. So much for growing wings. A hundred yards away, I spotted the frame of a scooter that the usual truants had dissected days ago. I pulled the remains of the bike against the wall, jumped on the saddle, and catapulted myself into the air.

On the other side of the wall, I took a moment to

catch my breath. Entombed in despair, I held my head in between the palms of my hands. Fear had stripped away the last piece of bravery in me. Soon after, I heard angry voices behind the wall.

That day, I was the most sought-after kid in the campus for all the wrong reasons.

On a warm spring afternoon, one supposedly "Barney & Friends" peaceful, I had been the victim of a heinous assault minutes after the bell had rung. I crawled home with my head gushing and my hand-me-down purple Lacoste soaked in a mixture of dried and fresh blood. Some dope-sniffing bullies from school had punished my buddy Rashid, and I stood up against the injustice, in blind temerity—stupidity would probably be a better choice of word here.

The "Terrible Trio," as we called them, went ballistic on the poor nerd because he had denounced their perpetual abuse to the school authority. Their unfair moral practice was met with sanctions including and up to expulsion. Rashid was rescued by the math teacher just in time, but I did not have such luck.

I was down to my last meal. Demolition was soon to begin.

The three vengeance-craving loonies caught up with me and dragged me in one of the underground parking lots situated at the basement of a nearby building. The place was empty during the early afternoon, which nullified any chance for an intervention.

At the helm of their opaque regime, Ahmed was the undisputed leader and also the oldest and strongest one. By no means less significant, the other two were nothing short of intimidating—all of them witless savages of unsavory reputation.

Archvillains to the nerds, they threatened anarchy across the neighborhood. If they were anywhere near the same ZIP code, the rest of us knew to exercise caution.

Not surprisingly, they were never more than one inch away from a life of corruption. The streets had hardened their spirits to the point of no return.

Their favorite pastime consisted of terrorizing fresh-off-the-boat students with a “Kick Me” sign posted on their back.

I had initially hoped for an amicable discussion over our issues instead of being pummeled to the ground, but Ahmed’s penchant for violence would not allow any chance at civility. I was subjected to a dangerous *mélange* of low IQ and arrogance.

It was downhill from there.

The inborn-evil hulk approached me, and while his accomplices held me down, he drove his massive right fist into the jelly of my belly. From the blow, the *choucroute* and the *foie gras* from lunch all vacated. I dropped on the floor from agony swaging like a headless snake.

Ahmed started to play soccer with my body while I lay on the floor blanketed in my own vomit. Even after I wet my pants, my merciless assailant went on with the punishment.

For a second, I could have sworn I heard the wailing of the Banshee.

Then in a desperate attempt, I bit one of the bullies who was holding me, and the pain made him release me from the constricted hold of his arms. It gave me a split second to act. I kicked Ahmed's Achilles' heel, and, as he hunkered over, I seized the occasion to push him to the ground. To very little surprise, my heroic action did not last very long before the other two grabbed me and threw me back onto the pavement.

Devil-possessed, Ahmed got up and rushed toward me. He lifted me off the ground with his hands closed around my neck like a monkey wrench.

"You pot-bellied pig, I'm gonna rearrange your face!"

"Heeeeeeeelp!" I screamed inarticulately as he choked me.

Then he struck me again.

"Cry now, *gros con*!" he screamed.

But I wouldn't give him the satisfaction. And just as it came, my fear disappeared. Almost immediately an in-surgence of rage came upon me. I clawed his arms with kitten fierceness and sprayed gushes of saliva and blood onto his pimpled-face and into his mouth.

Another fatal error.

His eyes lit up in pyromaniac's madness. The sclerae

turned red from fury with miniscule nerves swaying like larvae on the surface. Ahmed threw me like a sack of potatoes against the adjacent wall, and the back of my skull crashed against the rough surface of the cement.

As soon as I came in contact with the wall, I fell down hard on the asphalt but got up in no time. By the sound of the loud clash, my head must have been blown to bits. I felt no pain. At least, not yet.

"AhmedAAAA! You sucker! I'm not scared of you," I screamed in defiance, altering his name into a feminine form to mock him. In the projects, this was the worst possible form of insult anyone could inflict to any Algerian man, much less one with hardcore street hubris.

The raging bull inside of me provoked, I charged, huffing and puffing, in his direction, horns ahead and fear behind. Oddly enough, Ahmed broke into a peal of laughter and did nothing to parry the attack. The heartless bastard did not even have the decency to make me believe that he was a bit concerned.

I launched a salvo of punches onto his steel abs before he grabbed me by the collar and tossed me over his shoulder, using my own momentum against me. In that moment of rage, I totally forgot about all his warrior titles and would live to suffer the consequences. He was also the local champion in Judo, which explained in part his pugnacious spirit.

Immobile, I lay, barely breathing, on the ground for a moment. As I gathered pieces of myself together, I heard scurrying footsteps tapping away as in a situation of panic.

From afar, an old man saw the battery and honked repeatedly to scare off the hooligans. Much to my relief, it worked. In a flash, they disappeared into the unlit part of the gigantic parking area. I was left behind on the ground, face down. The old man helped me up and gave me a half-emptied bottle of Evian to wash the blood from my face. After checking the gash on my head, he offered to take me to the hospital to which I politely declined. I was dizzy but managed to walk. He insisted again, and I declined again.

In a minimum of time, he dropped me off in front of my apartment building. I thankfully saluted him with a nod and then crawled into the elevator. Inside, tenants stared at me with big wide eyes, even the old Asian man. Some were concerned, others disgusted. Most of them lived in the building so they were familiar with me, but I kept silent.

One of the tenants, an elderly woman better known as *La Sorciére* kept asking questions, to which I gave no answer. By then, the adrenaline rush was gone, replaced by the pain from the beating. Talking was the last thing on my mind. She did not understand and carried on with the interrogation. Filled with annoyance, I signaled her with a thumb up to let her know that I wasn't in such a bad shape as I looked. A lie, of course.

With the help of one of the other tenants, I wobbled out of the elevator. My vision started to blur. I held on to the wall for support and walked through the long corridor toward the door of my apartment unit—number twenty-one—never seemed so far off as on that day.

Inside, all the curtains were shut, and everything was quiet, but I knew Father was home. After his accident at work, he rarely stepped out of his room. I first went to the bathroom to wash up, and then I headed to his bedroom in search of comfort.

The room was inked in a Reaper's black. I could not see past the tip of my nose. There was no sound, not even the tick of a clock, only warm, stilled afternoon air. It took my eyes a second to adjust before I was able to discern the objects in front of me. Slowly, I swirled around them to avoid breaking my jaw on the floor, an injury I could not afford at that point.

I finally perceived my father's shape under the blanket. He was resting, peaceful as a starless sky without the cosmic commotion. Still holding a wet towel over the gash to suppress the bleeding, I sat next to him. I wanted to share with him my run-in with *Cerberus* but he was in a deep slumber, almost in a comatose state.

The discussion would likely be tabled for a later time, if at all.

A frequent dimensional journeyer, he was adrift in his own universe spiritually-wounded from a tragic past that would not let go of him. Wherever his soul might've been at that moment, I was in a much better place and better shape than he was.

Father stopped existing in our world, no more than we existed in his.

For the first time in my life, I witnessed his demons feast the light out of him. Seeing him in that state took my physical pain away. Quietly as not to wake him, I closed the door behind and cried for being so powerless and alone.

I needed comfort, but he needed more help than I would ever.

I understood that much about my life that day. It was a terrible reality that I could neither deny nor escape—a reality of lacking a fatherly figure. And nothing could save me from this indescribable feeling of inanition with the volume capacity of infinity.

Father died long ago in Nam.

Chapter 10

A Gust of Wind

The note read: *Meeting with the Principal today at three p.m. Be punctual.*

I recognized the fellow who served me by reputation. He was one of those sellout students whose dunce cap's marquee read: Prick of the Year. He seemed to pity me with his eyes, and I wanted to push my thumbs right through his pupils. Or perhaps that was just the way he looked at people. People like me, in particular.

The students summoned to the principal's office were usually up to their necks in trouble. That was just common knowledge. Nothing new here.

I was not fazed a bit.

All right, a little.

Twenty five minutes later, and still the principal was nowhere in sight. During his two-year tenure at that school, I saw the man only once during a speech he made in the auditorium about "Living Together in Peace & Equality," a slap in the face, by the general consensus. The subject matter was not part of a scheduled curricular activity. The event was necessitated after a group of students of Arab descent knifed two racially-hate-spewing skinhead students. The largest riot in the school history ensued. All classes were cancelled for two weeks straight, to my delight.

After the torrid tensions had subsided, the two skinheads grew their hair back and subscribed to another cult.

In the forefront, the office had a demilune reception area, in the back an untidy file storage unit with its door half-opened, and next to it the principal's lair or the "Red Chamber," as the students called it.

The overall décor suffered from a severe case of fashion faux-pas and desperately needed a touch of rejuvenation. The grotesque walls were painted in a depressing gray that did not sit well with the overly-abundant *caca d'oie* plastic plants. On each wall, hung gloomy abstract paintings of what appeared to be exotic birds. My best guess. But the cherry on top of the cake was the pervasive stench from the ink of the mimeograph. To the well-trained eye, the environment could have been purposely designed to discourage students from a second visit.

That last thought made me laugh silently inside.

His secretary, a tiny little old lady with self-dyed dark hair that made her look even older, told me to be patient. A virtue, she claimed. I normally would have leveled my eyes to hers out of courtesy, but the dark residue from the dye along her hairline caught my attention instead. Moved by an irresistible impulse, my lips came apart. It was one of those moments when resistance was futile, in spite of myself.

She was not amused.

"He must have had an important matter to tend to," she said in a professional manner while strangling me into unconsciousness with invisible giant hands that she had mentally conceived in that fraction of time.

The gleam in her eyes hinted to that conclusion.

"It's a good thing that one of us still respects punctuality," I replied, keeping a serious face.

Aggravated to the point of losing herself, she gave me the Robert De Niro stare and was about to make a comeback to redeem her boss when suddenly the main door opened. The principal walked in. He was a large abdominous man the size of door frames whose head was only separated from his body by a well-trimmed chinstrap that served as a line of demarcation.

He waved in my direction. "Step in my office, young man!" he ordered me in a deep voice.

The prideful man did not say anything else. He sat behind the humongous oak desk, the sole attribution of dignified power, and pulled my files out of the top drawer and plunged in revision for a brief moment, bespectacled.

Today promises to be a good day, I thought.

After he loosened his tie, he looked up and assessed me from head to toe as if he might uncover my true identity beneath. But I came prepared for those types of nonsense, all dressed-up à la Miami Vice.

"What would you like to do with your life?" he asked me.

In response, I tilted my head and elevated my shoulders as to say, *I'm not sure*.

That was the truth, I had no idea.

He continued the conversation by saying, "Look, young man, you produce very decent grades, especially in the linguistics department, but I'm afraid grades alone won't help you get through the next level."

I did not say a word, my gaze lost in the comically disturbing painting above his risible comb over.

His patience stretched thin. "Son, I am not entirely convinced you really understand the gravity of the situation," he added. "I've called upon you today because your attendance is as infrequent as a drop of rain in this heat. Precipitation reached a record low last month, if you follow me. Not to mention that one of your teachers is very vocal about you, in a very unflattering way."

"And what is the name of that mystery teacher?" I asked, as if doing so was my rightful entitlement to know my accuser for a proper defense. Although I knew exactly which teacher he was referring to all along.

"Well, your Economics teacher, Mr. Cauchon, isn't really thrilled with you. He charged that you only honored him of your presence for the exams," he said with a playful sarcastic tone. "Is there any reason why you have been missing so many days, or should I say weeks?"

I looked at him and answered in a stern and elevated voice, "Mr. Cauchon does not like my kind!" As soon as I spoke up, I knew it was a bad choice of inflection.

Taken aback by my retort, he became silent for a moment overcome by the combative spirit I had demonstrated. An implosion in his mind occurred. He expected a small little voice from a person of my stature.

He followed, matching my tone, "*Pauvre Diable!* I would be careful if I were you. That's some serious allegation here!" He wiped the pearls of sweat off his dripping forehead.

This time, I replied in a more respectable voice. "I'm only speaking the truth, and it sure doesn't matter whether you believe me. Mr. Cauchon told me on numerous occasions that my life will never change, regardless of my education."

He looked at me, this time straight in the eyes. "At the end of the day, it's your absences that speak louder. You did not show up to class so you will face the consequences."

"And, what are the consequences?" I asked, with irritation showing now in my speech—tremor and spit.

"I have no choice, and it is also by the recommendation of Mr. Cauchon, but to hold you back this year. Sorry but there's nothing else I can do for you. You may appeal to the Board of Education if you please."

I kept to myself for a minute.

An image of Maman carrying me on her back in the old country came to mind. My failure would be hers as well, and she did not deserve that. She would have a heart attack.

Adding to my depression, I faced an eternal struggle with her. She insisted I become a doctor, or something of that rank, while I wanted none of that. My passion resided with writing, but she argued that I could never get to the second page of a chapter book without dozing off. She had a good case, but science just was not my strong suit.

Then I asked, for clarification. "What about my classmate Gaston GrosNez?"

"What about Mr. GrosNez?" he demanded.

"Well, his attendance is the real drought, and my grades are far better than his by a milestone. So, why is it that he is allowed to move forward?"

"Monsieur GrosNez is not the focus of this discussion, and none of your concern to begin with," he replied with an annoyed tone.

I'd pinched a nerve.

I fired back with an incendiary response. "I beg to differ, sir, but he is. The only difference is that his father sits on the panel of the Board of Education."

A morbid pause.

The silence grew oppressive.

I remained firm on a stand of principle and proceeded. "This will not be left unspoken at the hearing. Everyone will get their comeuppance."

He gave me an intense look. Then finally, he said, "This meeting is adjourned. Good luck to you, son."

"I'm not your son!"

I stormed out of the office. The secretary kept her eyes fixed on the typewriter, the invisible giant hands buried deep in her mind.

While on the public transit during the short trip home, a million thoughts assailed my mind. Restlessly, I was plotting on how to confront Maman.

On my left, sat an old man who looked like he had just come out of a low-budget zombie flick. The yellow hue that enveloped his worn-out clothes faded into a pale white, and his gray hair was shiny from the unwashed scum.

It did not matter. He seemed nice.

It was also the only available spot.

Then he asked me, "Kid, do you know the time?"

I looked at my watch, and he said, "No, not this time."

I had no clue and remained silent.

He smiled and said, "It's time to be happy, young man."

And as the last word slipped out of his lips, he got off at his stop.

On that same day, important news came in unexpectedly and left us *bouche bée*. It wasn't so much the news that came as a shock but the manner in which it was relayed. Maman came home from work earlier than usual, which was already an indication. She drank half a bottle of red wine, another strong indication, and she did not bother to check with the little guy.

That was the selling point.

She simply said in a thunderous voice, "Kids, we are leaving to America by the end of summer!"

Maman's family had petitioned for us to join them ever since the very first year we debarked on the French shoreline, but she had kept the matter secretive until now. It all made sense. She had never been the same after her first visit there some years ago. A revelation, she declared. To be frank, I've never seen her more excited about anything since the nomination of Pope John Paul II.

There was no protestation on my end.

Besides, I did not have any friends or anything of importance to hold onto. And because it aroused a sort of inward joy, a personal victory, it seemed a good idea all the more. Sometimes it's best to put the past in the rear-mirror.

That night I dreamed of the mouthwatering *milles-feuilles* and *puits d'amour*, the few things I would truly miss.

Chapter 11

Fields of Tulips

As I lay awake, tossing and turning, the aroma of brewed freshly-ground coffee drew me out to the balcony of the seventh-floor studio apartment situated in the outskirt of the thirteenth arrondissement of central Paris. A denizen of the night, my soul was in sorest travail from the rhythmically homogeneous crescendo of sirens and passenger trains rolling against the rails.

Under normal circumstances, the exhaustion from the trip would have pinned my eyes shut, but this was an exception. The excitement of being in the City of Light was the component of difference.

Months earlier, I had made plans to visit my sister,

the fashion designer, who had lived there for five years now.

Toto, the cat, followed me outside to share a view of the Seine River where a line-up of *Péniches-à-louer* awaited the first waves of sightseeing tourists. My personal favorite was the *Arc-de-Triomphe* for its emblematic representation of history, and in my humble opinion the real enlightenment of the city. The Romanesque-inspired architecture was located a few blocks away from where I was standing. Bellow my feet, a bewilderment of people embarked for another manic Monday.

Shortly after taking her habitual morning shower, my sister came out to the balcony and handed me the phone. "C'est, Maman!" she said in a trembling voice.

Maman requested my immediate return. She insisted to only tell me the reason face-à-face before the line went dead.

The matter had been shrouded in secrecy, but it was clearly a presage of bad omen in progress. That thought sent a shiver of icebergs through my body.

My vacation was short-lived, but I complied without resistance. For clarification, hara-kiri would have been wiser a choice over a skirmish with my mother. And so, against my will, I jumped on the next available train. During the nightmarish seven-hour ride, I attempted to shake off all the pessimistic thoughts with little success while exorbitant weariness corkscrewed deeper into my mind.

To my surprise, my mother met me at the train station alone.

Upon greeting me, she remained mute the whole time as if there was nothing to say. The dreadful silence, an apparent concomitant conspirator of hers, engendered the short drive home the equivalency of those long seven hours of torture in the train. When we arrived at home, the atmosphere did not alleviate the tenseness of the situation either. The apartment was empty, filled with an unfamiliar feeling and reeking of the scent of burning incense.

Mother remained distraught. After a short while, she went to the kitchen to recover a serving of pastries. By the look in her gaze, she was terrified to tell me something of importance. I was growing impatient by the moment and took umbrage at her unusual behavior. I pushed the pastries aside with the back of my hand and said, "Enough. I want an answer."

She attempted an evasive answer but had a second thought before it even ended. After taking a deep breath, she held my hands tightly and finally spoke up with a newly-found controlled composure.

"Lucas is dead!"

Bullet to my brain, then blank. My right leg started to shake frantically out of nervousness, and without looking at her, I replied, "What are you talking about? And which Lucas? I know just about ten Lucases, if not more," I told her in an incredulous tone.

"Your Lucas," she replied in a broken voice with brimming eyes.

A pause.

The horror of understanding and putting the last piece of evidence together sank in finally. Overtaken by rage, I yelled out, "Impossible! I just talked to him last week. He is to be married in two months. I should know. I am the best man. I was in Paris to get my tuxedo. Don't you do that to me!"

I ignored her words, and, refusing to listen to the rest of the story, I stormed out to fill my mind with more blanks. But the recitals of my mother's words kept rolling inside.

Lucas is dead.

Your Lucas.

That year, while working as a scoutmaster in Provence, Lucas drowned after he'd rescued a boy from the Argens River. The headline of the local newspaper labeled his accidental death as a confluence of events pinpointed by tragedy at the intersection.

According to the authorities, his heavy camper boots drew him quickly into the depth of the murky water and did not allow him to resurface. It was believed that the exhaustion from the rescue attempt proved too much. He struggled gravely until death came unto him, the autopsy report stated. Lucas became a hero overnight through his courageous action. A posthumous medal would be issued to honor his bravery. But none of that mattered.

Nothing would bring him back.

How can one make sense of any of this? Unless you have a crystal ball, there is no way to anticipate those tragic moments that life sometimes delivers at your doorstep, I thought in disbelief.

I coiled in indelible grief, embittered by the cruelty inflicted upon us all.

Lucas was the closest thing to a real brother to me, one who truly cared for me. He possessed a wondrous personality and always helped others, even if it meant making personal sacrifices on his part. Hordes of followers eternally gravitated about him like bits of Saturn's belt. What they admired most was his inhumanely nobleness of the mind. This was what he was all about in distilled essence.

That most beautiful man had changed my life for the better in every way possible. He instilled in me the joy of genuine fellowship and brotherhood. Because of his constant support, I was able to find some sort of peace from my traumas.

In the Kingdom of the Lord, he was one of a kind with no precedence.

Unlike what most people felt, it wasn't so much his death that troubled me but the life he could have had, all wasted in a dismal twist of fate. These thoughts haunted me without end. I rejected my pain and remained in denial up until I saw his lifeless corpse inside the casket.

Everyone took notice of the somber expression on

his face. For the first time, he seemed unhappy. "Gone too soon," all whispered under their breath.

The layer of cosmetics and embalming were unsuccessful in their task. So as not to distress the children with the sight of his corpse, Aunt May ordered the coffin of her only child shut. Hundreds of people flocked to the funeral service to pay him a last tribute. I was present only for a moment at the wake proper.

The following day, I did not attend the burial.

I preferred to mourn alone.

Sensing my distress, Mémé approached me one morning. "Only real men cry, my young one. So let it all out, for only then the healing process may begin. Let it all out."

That day I finally cried in solitude.

Endless rivulets.

After Lucas's passing, I avoided both his fiancée and especially his mother. Almost every day, Aunt May awaited by the window for my visit, and in so doing only compounded her misery. But I stayed away. My presence would be a catalyst for more pain and multiply the outcome exponentially, I thought—a constant reminder.

Also, I couldn't bear the sight of her slipping away in the clutches of despair. Being so young at the time, I had neither the knowledge nor the strength to console her anymore. We all struggled to find a life beyond his death.

I had not been spared.

Most of all, I could not reconcile with the sentiment of giving her false hope.

It wasn't long until she fell gravely ill, fretted with dark-ringed eyes wide open but unseeing. The doctor diagnosed a bacterial infection of bowels, which led to extreme fatigue and a loss of appetite.

She was only suffering from an afebrile case of broken heart.

Tulips in hand, I visited her once at the hospital and never returned.

As selfish as it sounds, there was an element of relief when I set sail for America at the end of summer that same year. I bade her no farewell. I was convinced it was for the better.

In the wake of a spiritual enlightenment two decades of torment later, I finally mustered enough courage to go back to France to visit Aunt May. There was no point to my reluctance anymore.

Unsure about her reaction, I decided to make the trip unannounced. After all these years of cowardice, there was a possibility she might deny me visitation. Shame could have such paranoid effect on anyone.

There was only one way to find out.

That Sunday morning, riven by contrary impulses, I stood frozen in front of her door. All the memories and all the pain came back with a vengeance.

Both my feet were planted deeply in the past, and as much as I tried to ignore those thoughts, they established permanent residency in my mind. Where peace was expected, I found uneasiness instead.

Something in me was deeply troubled. I felt my throat constrict.

Tongue-tied behind the door, I scrambled for the right words to say. I had played out that meeting in my mind thousands of times on the plane, and there I was, stupefied and unsure of what to do.

Unable to push forward, I sat on the steps of the porch and watched the steady flow of passing cars with passengers mostly showing crash-test-dummies expression on their faces. In Indian file, some kids waved at me and sauntered across the muddy lawn in hurried strides. Their laughter soon echoed in the distance.

A moment passed, slow and dull. The thought of leaving crossed my mind. It would be a lot easier on both of us. It was hard to reconnect with that part of my past that was left behind long ago. Then without warning, I felt a hand on my shoulder.

Aunt May was standing right behind me.

I remembered that familiar touch. We both cried, she openly, me quietly inside.

"I knew you'll come back someday," she said in a soft voice. "I never gave up hope."

"I'm sorry if it took me this long, I was…" I searched for words again.

"There's no need for an apology," she reassured me with a voice only reserved to me, it seemed. "I understand your reason. I was just worried about you."

Eyes rimmed red, we held each other in silence. Two decades had disappeared in a painful blink.

At first light the very next day, I drove off deep in the highlands of the *Alpes de Haute Provence*, to pay respect to Lucas. Throughout our brotherhood, he had always mentioned that there was no other scenery as magnificent as the rainbow fields of tulips that enclosed the small village of his childhood. The wedding was set to be held there.

He was buried nearby instead.

That morning, amid the graciously-choreographed movements of the rainbow tulips dancing in the wind and the serenity of that heavenly place on earth, I felt the distinct sensation of his spiritual presence all around me.

Magnificent was an understatement.

Chapter 12

Sunshine

Saint Valentine's Day came full circle on a Sunday that year, and it brought along another cause for celebration—my daughter's very first birthday.

That morning, I got up earlier than usual and took a quick sailor-shower in order to get the final preparations for the birthday party underway. At daybreak, her mother, Mona, was still sleeping. She'd never been an early bird to be fair, but working the late shift the night before provided her with a plausible argument.

That point of contention did not ruffle my feathers a bit. It didn't matter. I could not sleep past sunrise for the life of me. That's a routine I have come to appreciate for peace of mind.

For the occasion, we had invited few friends and mostly family members with their entire colonies. By noon, the place was jammed with kids disguised as fairy tale characters, running around and destroying the manicured lawns with their tiny feet.

All things considered, the party was a success, except that I had been scolded because I forgot the damn piñata.

"She is too small to beat on it anyway," I said in my defense.

By the look of utter revulsion on Mona's face, it did not sit well with her. This was the sort of matter that required no further discussion. I quickly outpaced my shadow in the opposite direction to avoid direct confrontation and mostly being massacred.

After a whole afternoon of distributing *Tres Leches* cakes and supervising the tribe of rascals, I took a well-deserved break on a bench in the far end of the terrace. From there, I observed my baby girl, a constant smile on her face, showing her first two central incisors in ebullient frolic. The youngest among the children, she mimed everyone with utter frustration because her Bambi legs could not catch up fast enough with her desire to run.

In a not-so-distant past, I recalled the day of delivery at the hospital. It was a bit comical at the beginning. The nurse herded out Mona's mother and allowed only Maman to join us in the room. I did not quite understand the reason, but that was the least of my concern, perhaps due to her family's constant grousing about our parenthood out of wedlock. They were very traditional. My folks more lenient, to the exclusion of Mother.

For months, we had debated but could not agree on a name that we approved of mutually, and time had just run out. The labor lasted roundly nine hours and finally our daughter was introduced to her first ray of light in the early morning.

All seven and a half pounds of pure delight, she was a miniature carbon copy of Mona.

Seeing those tiny little ET-like fingers reaching out for the first time was a transformative moment. Her beautiful kiss-me lips let out a sleepy yawn while her eyelids were serenely shut, tired from the long journey.

When I held her for the first time, after she was taken out of the bassinet, she made my world a better place instantly. Her smile brought the first sign of light into my darkness. She was the prettiest little girl in the world and words I would have had with anyone who disagreed.

In that moment of rejoicing, I finally found a name for her: *Iris.*

For some inexplicable reasons, the faces of three wonderful classmates of mine in high school sharing that same name popped in my head—a sign, I began to believe. To this end, I have never told her mother about the reason behind the name.

Mea Culpa.

This represented the very first time I was truly happy. It was in fact Iris who gave me the gift of life again that day.

In the evenings, while her mother worked late hours, we watched reruns of Seinfeld. Her favorite character was Kramer for the crazy hair, and mine was George for his over-the-top neurotic behaviors.

During most of her waking hours, she would rarely make a sound as though to give me a moment to myself. To my slothful relief, she only cried when soiled but never out of whim. Along the way, her eternal smile acquired her of the nickname "Sunshine." Her good spirit made all the difference in my world as I drew my strength through her vitality. At that stage of my life, my whole joy was centered within her.

In the meantime, my relationship with her mother was on the verge of a collapse. From an outward standpoint, things appeared to be normal but reality depicted a different picture. If we had hoped that the birth of our daughter would jump-start our love, we were overly ambitious. I had long suspected this would not hold up in practice. Our life had been subjected to such ebbs and flows for quite some time.

Cited irreconcilable, at least on my end, the real issues mainly rooted from the ardor of youth and a lack of experience in life, never mind love. At war with one another for the most part, we also had to confront the great contrast between our personalities. Our relationship originated from an impassable divide that couldn't bridge the physical attraction to something of more substance—ephemeral lusts mistaken for love.

Adding to our own issues, I grew tired of her father's constant involvement in every aspect of our life. Still, she refused to acknowledge his detrimental effect on us—denial would be the clinical term for such behavior. In his defense, she insisted that he knew better. The old man was a self-righteous doctor, so my opinions were not even considered secondary. It was a losing battle.

Mona felt the steady withdrawal in me, but ever hopeful, she ignored her foreboding. On my end, I couldn't disguise my detachment, nor did I try. I spent less and less time in her company.

After all these years together, I had never opened up to Mona. I was still the *inconnu* she'd met long ago. She did not know who I really was inside and would never for that matter. Nobody did at that point.

Something had changed the scope of my emotions. I felt differently about her and I was distant from that point on. No matter how hard she tried, I drifted farther away. Our propinquity, sitting on thin ice, was not what it once was. She finally recognized the futility of her intentions when realizing that I'd reached the point of no return. It did not matter. I no longer attached any importance to the notion of "us" anymore.

Iris was my only reason to stay.

A few weeks earlier, Mona had been promoted to a managerial position that also required a change in scenery. She assumed the job without consulting with me, again. She had thought it would be a good idea for the three of us to just disappear into some exotic place far away. I made no effort to object when the news was finally brought to my attention. *It's not the location but the people*, I disagreed mentally.

This presented the perfect occasion to break away from her.

My only concern was my daughter.

With daddy on her side, Mona would fight me tooth and nail for her custody, a sure thing. I was not intimidated a bit. I just had a different view on life and everything else.

Despite my stronger bond with Iris, the laws of nature offered me no ground for protestation. She needed her mother more at that age. Inspired by that belief, I knew it'd be best for Mona to retain physical custody.

But no matter the outcome, I ruined her life. The guilt of being unable to provide a happy home with both parents under the same roof for her was uncontainable.

I had failed my daughter.

Already I was overcome with panic. Not knowing if Iris would be well treated and welcomed in a new household was undoubtedly my worst nightmare. The worse to happen never seemed of much a possibility until now.

To even consider that I would not be around twenty-four/seven anymore to protect her from any injustice of life became a depressing subject matter. I found no comfort in my thoughts, just insidious fear and more fear. That powerless feeling weighed on me like a sentence.

Born into conflict, she was barely one year old and so fragile. How could I ever let anyone else take care of her? Why did I ever bring this beautiful soul into this cruel world? And how could I possibly live without her eternal smile? Tens of thousands of staggering questions filled my petrified mind.

All of my childhood traumas came back to revisit me, one by one. Reprimanded in paralysis, I feared that something similar would happen to her, and the cycle of traumas would be passed on onto her. And this time it was all my doing.

No one else to blame.

There was no qualm in shielding me from guilt. Only the future would portend of her fate when all the circumstances would align. At that point, all I could do was to regroup and accept the situation.

Braving my inner struggle, I had been embattled with the idea of ending our union and the thought seemed more attractive by the days. I had sought this separation secretly to find the right words to say at the right moment. Almost half a year had gone by since then, but recently the truth had become too big a burden I neither had the will nor the strength to carry any longer.

That cold day on the bench, I knew the end of us was nearing. A voice surged from the depths of my reason and screamed for liberation.

Still, I couldn't find in my heart to push forward with the plan and tried to convince myself to wait for the next rain to tell her. The rain would probably make things easier for me, I kept thinking.

Maman often told me that when I was a kid, I would always stay outside to enjoy the rain until my clothes were all drenched. One time I even got bed-ridden from a pneumatic attack. She could not make sense of my infatuation with the rain, but she knew that somehow it made me happy. So she let it be because happy has never been a prevalent source in my life.

After a long silence, as if for dramatic emphasis, the final verdict came in. The torrential descent of our relationship could not be stopped anymore with a few sandbags of false hope. There was a sudden urge to vocalize my emotions—rain or not.

Iris was the only link between us, and she could not ever be the only reason to hold us together. Soon or later, she would understand that her life had been corroded by her parents' nonexistent love. And if we left this lie unchallenged, she would hurt much more someday.

Experience has taught me that the hardest part was not to part ways but actually to stay and pretend to be happy. This was by far the most difficult decision I ever had to make in my entire life.

"You may hate me for this, but something has been weighing heavily on my mind," I said.

Chapter 13

Amistad

It was late May in the year of yet another El Niño's tumultuous passage when I was introduced to my good old friend Don during a banquet held at the family ranch. My impression of him upon our first encounter left me inundated with an indescribable feeling of *je ne sais quoi.*

Quite a character in his own right, he wore his hair in a butt cut with two uneven over-processed bangs that lengthened past his chin. On his shoulders rested sprinkles of white residues from the excessive use of hair products that could have been mistaken for dandruffs.

In contrast with his tiny frame, his pants were ample enough to fit another person—he was scrawny beyond words. But much more than all that, it was the grotesque colors of his clothes that were the main attraction. He was sporting a lurid orange shirt with thin horizontal black stripes and some pinstripe bright lemon pants held by suspenders borrowed from Steve Urkel.

The very sight of him creased everyone's crows' feet but no one dared say a thing, at least not in front of him, too busy dealing with the sharp pain in their ribcage. It wouldn't be a stretch of the imagination to say that every single person present that day, old and young, pelted him with unflattering thoughts.

The only thing missing in this humorous high-octane display of chutzpah was the town crier to announce his arrival.

The real tragedy in all this, I must admit, was that the poor soul did not seem preoccupied by his outré sartorial taste and paraded without any self-consciousness as if to campaign for a cult of personality. In spite of it, I marveled at his unquestionable ability to ignore what people thought of him. That must have taken quite some strength and a thick skin.

After an afternoon watching him ridiculed by the other guests, even among the supposedly mature adults, who went as far as suggesting that his clothes were the products of donation, I surged to his defense by taking him away for a tour of the ranch.

Seemingly polar opposites, Don was a proud and boastful spirit, whereas I was selectively social, which is none but a more sophisticated way to describe the state of being introverted. Humility was not a familiar term in his vocabulary as I found out, but being his junior I forgave him any lapses in decorum—cultural constraints might've played a role here.

Due to these characteristic differences, our friendship did not fully blossom until I finally came to terms with the embers of his cantankerous persona, although his outlandish choice of style has never failed to pull the muscles in the corners of my mouth.

Down the road, I noticed his uncontrollable temper regardless of the gravity to any situation. One minute he was the frail alter ego, and the next, he metamorphosed into this depraved creature. As much as I thought of him as an immature scoundrel of the first order, a Prima Donna by definition, I also saw something good in him. There was a certain kindness in his eyes that came from a warm place so well hidden that one would have to spend enough time in his company to see it. I felt some undeniable strength and a strong will emanating from within his stick-figure frame. And quickly, I discarded all his flaws—dealing with mine was already an overly strenuous effort.

Secretively inside, I admired his bold audacity. I was certain that all he needed was an attentive ear. A true friend.

Mise-à-part his unpredictable stormy temperament, Don was a fun person to be around, always seeking for the next escapade. It took some time, but eventually he vaulted into a higher order of privilege in my book after I became habituated to his way of living. The prospect of long-term fellowship had never been upon us up to that point.

As night-and-day as we were, he somehow started to fill a portion of Lucas' spot. And so began our slow collision into friendship.

The seasons rolled on by to find Don as lonely as a fish in a bowl until one day he met the love of his life. So enthused was he that all the four corners of the world echoed of his conquest. The object of much wide-eyed adulation, she had his heart pulsating in the palm of her hands.

I felt so much frisson of excitement out of him that it got me worried, yet I couldn't help but rejoice silently for him. Out of everyone, he deserved to be happy.

Her name was Carmen and she was by all means, an attractive *demoiselle* far beyond his league which got me even more worried. If anything, he was not a stark realist—had never been one to what I knew of him so far. I wasn't sure whether to applaud his bravery or to give him a piece of advice. If not I, then who else? It was the kind of situation that could change the narrative of an entire life, but I knew my effort would be at odd with Don's legendary obstructionism and intransigence. So I kept my feeling unspoken.

On that first meeting at the local bar, she appeared as

an enchantress with a fire-retardant heart that no rules of love would apply to. To the common mortal, a man-eater. But looks could be deceiving. I regrouped, guilt-ridden for having such negative vibes about her.

Then one sweat-drenching day when the tedium of the early evening became too much to bear, Don asked me to accompany him to Carmen's work place. After a brief hesitation, I agreed. My ration of cigarettes was running low, and I knew it wouldn't last me through the night.

Once there, I quickly regretted my decision. As I was waiting for him, the screen of stale hot air made me want to break my face on the steering wheel.

I spent the next fifteen minutes puffing doughnuts of smoke inside the A.C-deprived rusty metallic-gray station wagon—a real chick magnet. In those glory days of our youth, we'd picked up mostly chicas, mainly because I could pass for Latino with my resembling features and that bronze sun-parched tan skin.

The white girls wanted nothing to do with our ride.

After a few more moments, Don looked in my direction to confirm my attention and beckoned to me with one arm to hurry over. Without much concern, I walked over to him in a laid-back cowboy sort of way, in my flip-flops. Carmen had wished to speak to me about a possible double-date with one of her friends. While I was talking to her, he disappeared into the convenience store three doors down.

What came next left me bereft of words.

"I would like to get to know you better," Carmen confessed.

Just like that, she drove a stake through his heart. Don, who had not the faintest idea, went back to the car and played some old New Wave ballads on the stereo.

The situation was far from acceptable. Far.

Confused and mostly disgusted, I demanded. "Why are you misleading my brother? Do you not know how he feels about you?"

"We're just friends," was her swift response. "I really like your dark sense of humor *et surtout* that bizarre way how you express yourself." She giggled. "That's such a turn on."

"Over-My-Dead-Body," I told her, despite feeling flattered.

Locked in a duel of intense stares, we drowned our words in silence.

Try as I might, I could not reverse the high blood psi from arising. Desultorily, I walked back to the car, all in turmoil, and told Don to slide over to the passenger side. He nodded his head as to say okay and "What's going on?" simultaneously.

I offered no answer pretending that I had not read the expression on his face.

I slammed the door shut and drove the gas pedal to the metal.

On the way back home, I kept my eyes fixed on the

road in tunnel vision spreading clouds of dust and blasting *Enter Sandman* to the max. The hot wind on my face made me want to drive even faster. On a normal day, fifteen minutes on the freeway would have sufficed to get back home. Not that day. I took another deserted stretch with a better view of the arid country side—El Niño was long gone by then. All we could see, in all direction, were plain fields of dirt and more dirt that reached the blurred line of the horizon caused by heatwaves that separated infinity from the earth.

Wrapped in thoughts, I was biting my tongue from telling him of what had just transpired. During the whole time, I was wrestling with my mind. I kept the music loud so I wouldn't have to improvise an answer or even a lie.

I played the song over and again inexhaustibly. Don did not say a word. Normally, he would be in my face after the third replay. In the past, he'd tossed some of my CDs out of the window for lesser reasons—to my regret to this day, I should have returned the favor with those old New Wave albums. It's amazing how a few years in age difference could translate into a whole generation gap in music. I abhorred his sentimental taste. Period.

Some situations required the fierce electrical guitar element to drown out the noise inside. That's what I needed at that moment. Not some depressing and cheesy ballads. That last thought made me smile, which drew more confusion in him.

I kept on playing the same song, and still he showed

no symptoms of frustration. That was telling me something.

Perhaps he just wanted to let me be. Or perhaps he knew. She might've alluded something about it to him earlier. And that wasn't a bad thing. If that were the case, I would not have to explain it to him after all. Sometimes an explanation might be perceived as an act of guilt, I thought.

But his comportment did not appear to reflect any sense of awareness on the matter. I was the messenger boy—the bearer of bad news.

By the time we reached the farm it was dark. Not hungry himself, he skipped dinner. I devoured two servings of Maman's best traditional food, ginger and beef sautéed in oyster sauce over vermicelli and minced-lemongrasses premixed with tofu, accompanied by a shrimp paste-based papaya salad and killer red hot chili peppers—and sticky rice, of course.

After a session of newspaper reading in the oval office, to buy time obviously, I joined him in the back of the barn by the old eucalyptus tree. Our spot. By then he had already started a bonfire, nova bright and cracking.

After killing half of the bottles of borrowed-booze that my brother Hercules had clandestinely stashed in the basement, I couldn't hold off my tongue much longer.

There was no use of an atomistic approach to this issue, I realized. Being inebriated would probably make it easier on both of us also.

So I thought.

Showing momentary panic, I revealed verbatim, for transparency and concision, Carmen's true intention. "She confessed earlier that she would like to get to know me better. And I told her, over-my-dead-body."

A pause.

"I'm afraid she is not that into you. Sorry, bro."

"What else did she say?" he asked, stunned by the revelation.

"She said that she only sees you as a friend."

"What else?" His voice started to show frustration.

"Just let it be, man. That lady is bad news."

Silence.

Things went from peaceful to horrific in a nick of time. The news set his anger ablaze. Heart thundering, his cheeks burned from mortification. His nostrils flared up the size of two jumbo black olives. His eyes lit up instantly in magenta madness as his feelings stirred in a cocktail of frustration and rage.

Such an outburst would do more harm than good—the poor bastard nearly had a coronary. It became clear to me that he would not survive the rejection with his pride unscathed. From all accounts, I had seen once too many times that rage yet never to that extent. He shuddered from the intense emotional quake for failing to win over her affection.

The alcohol might've had something to do with that also.

"Take it easy, bud!" I yelled out. "Snap out of it, would you? She's never promised you the moon."

Ironically, the night was pitch black.

Then in panting breaths and without batting an eyelash, he whimpered, "I'm wounded but not dead—"

As soon as those words were spoken, I knew that I bore witness to a precipice of *colère* at hand, a never-ending story.

Don was suffering a tragic case of *duende* in which love was not reciprocal. This marked the cessation of his brain function for the rest of the night and for a long while.

More than anything, I wanted to preserve our brotherhood from a collapse to which he thanked me for my loyalty. She was capable of such abomination.

But all things considered, I couldn't hold Carmen accountable for it. She was entitled to her own choice. He had no relevance in her heart, no more than a constituent had to an incumbent. For that reason alone, I would not allow myself any ill-feelings toward her. Don was what concerned me. He was infatuated with her, and deliverance just became a matter of fiction, an encumbrance which would lessen any chance at recovery.

After seething in silence for a moment, he asked for closure. "There is no need for closure here," I explained. "There has to be a relationship to begin with for those kind of things to make sense."

This was not the sort of operatic tragedy that involved the loss of true love.

This was a case of lust, plain and simple. The only thing I could do was to give him unsolicited advices on how to approach the situation and move on. One step at a time. Trying to wring a smile out of him, I repeated his own words back to him, "There's plenty of fish in the ocean. All you need is…you know…"

He chuckled, but a pretend smile reduced to a grimace caught in the reflection of the faint light on his face suggested otherwise—the very depiction of low spirits.

With veins throbbing at his temples, Don was unresponsive to my jokes after that point. His mind clearly elsewhere, he remained still and kept his gaze on the fire making a point of ignoring me. His silence was indicator of the heaviness of the situation. He seemed beyond saving.

This sudden convulsion of thunderous clouds above our serenity had changed our existence in more ways than intended.

I felt the bitterness. I knew him for not accepting defeat lightly. I knew him to be competitive. I knew him being stronger.

That day, I saw no trace of any of that.

There was no relief in sight.

For the first time, Don was out in the open and vulnerable. He looked possessed at best and half dead at worst. And that was not a bit exaggerated.

That vain machismo cloak had been a false advertisement of his character all along. The pretend front had been hidden his self-identity from his own consciousness for as long as he lived. I had not been fooled. This was one of those rare exceptions when the book could be judged by its cover. The real Don was still a frightened kid in search of a personality and a place to belong. He was after recognition and wished to prove to all that there was more to him than appearance suggested.

For the greater part of our friendship, I never thought any less of him. I accepted him as a brother, and that was all that mattered. Being the closest person to him, I had hoped that he would redefine himself and find liberation from his insecurities on his own term someday.

In the early morning, we emptied the case of Heineken and also two bottles of Merlot, out of necessity. We lay comatose on the *chaises lounges*, eyes rolled far back in our heads, leaving the ground bleeding purple from the tipped-over bottles.

The mighty Hercules wasn't having it that morning.

This type of cases involving rejection was never simple to treat spiritually. The only cure is time. Having your heart broken stays with you for a very long time—in many cases, even after a replacement has come along and mended it. But what do I know? My heart was in a million pieces as well, probably in worse shape than his.

Day after day, the brilliance of madness in his eyes faded away in gradual phases. I was not entirely convinced, however. I had heard that song before. Beneath the calm water I felt the fury quietly conspiring.

With perseverance, I continued to give him emotional support and implored him to move on—those first weeks had been a whirlwind. Instead, he detached slowly away from our bond and would not avail himself for any type of dialogue anymore. I understood. Somehow I was part of the source of his grief. Sorely vexed, he needed time alone. He had been on life-support ever since that night.

The months went by, and still he remained at large without leaving word as to his whereabouts.

I was as lonely as a fish in a bowl.

That same year, Don came by one day, arm-in-arm with Carmen, in total exultation as though nothing had happened. By the wild gleam in his eyes, I could tell it was his supreme moment. Apparently, he'd failed to stay away from her and begged for a relationship. He wanted her submission. She took possession of his instead.

It's almost biologically impossible to be that naïve, I thought.

In this spirit, he must have played his card right and earned that one-in-a-million chance she'd allow any suitor that lacked potential out of pity. Women would do that. Men, not so much. But I could be wrong.

This was one of those moments, I feared, where winning would have a far worse effect on his psyche when reality settled. Still, he was only guilty of being mercilessly weak from a loss of intellectual coherence.

Apparently, his evident distrust in me had turned him against my warning. How could one make good on the promise of loyalty under the watchful eye of temptation? I should have seen it coming. He was already too far emotionally invested to get out of it.

Doubly disturbed that I had not pressed for an explanation, he offered me one. "Don't worry! I know what I'm doing," he whispered to me.

To which I responded, "Someday it may not be sufficient a reason."

He clearly suffered from a dislocation from reality which might've trickled his fancy.

Along this line, he attempted further explanation but I did not give him a chance. He was beyond persuasion, and I had no wish to waste any more time on that matter.

We avoided any mention of the incident thereafter.

Another year went by before they were married. By then they were also expecting their first child. I was appointed the best man's duty but respectfully declined, a decision I had to live by. Ever since Lucas's death, I had vowed to myself to never assume that responsibility again.

Don was offended, despite the fact that I had always been clear about this matter. This would only set us apart further.

Not long after the wedding, they moved back to Eau Claire, Wisconsin, to care for his ailing mother in her dotage. I would be lying to say that his departure did not affect me.

Beyond that point, we did not keep much contact. Along with them the commotion was gone. My life found a new normal, a banality well-appreciated.

A few years later, they conceived two more children and seemed happy from what my sources told me on occasions. Into the fifth year, she pulled the plug on their marriage and ran off. It was rumored that his temper got the very best of their marriage after years of being emasculated. Eventually, the breakup came as no surprise to anyone but him. We all knew that she did him a great disservice by marrying him.

Up to that point, I had kept silent, knowing that it was just a matter of time before he'd contact me. So I waited patiently. One month, two…and another season came along.

Then one day while I was on vacation, he finally let down his pride and called me with an undertone of desperation. He needed comfort from his torments.

From the beginning of their marriage, I knew that he was bound to make that phone call one day. Yet, I felt deeply remorseful for the accuracy of my prediction.

On a positive note, my knowledge of what would occur had prepared me to shoulder the kind of responsibility needed to help my good old friend when the occasion arose.

Against my up-bringing, I took pity on the pulseless

man, and I spent the next five months trying to remedy his sufferings. I did not want him to turn up in an emergency room due to alcohol poisoning and an overdose of depression which was the likelihood of what could have happened.

Mostly he regretted not listening to me and admitted that all his misfortunes had befallen him because of his blind love for her. I advised him to focus on his children instead. They should always come first, although we couldn't escape the conclusion that this was, for all its struggles, the beginning of a hard life for them.

I had not felt the benefit of an entire night's sleep during the following months, but I continued to show patience and support regardless. I wasn't exactly a beacon of wisdom but being a single father myself made me better able to relate to his situation. Love was certainly not a place where we had both excelled.

As his closest friend, it was in my duty and responsibility to protect him from himself. Any mishandling on my part would ensure his spiritual demise. Besides, he did not have that many friends either. Don had that intricacy in his personality that made anyone either love or hate him. In this case, the latter inclination significantly outweighed the former.

Nothing could have helped insulate him from despair. The poor man was utterly lost and called me around twenty-four/seven. That's what I had to deal with in the days, weeks, and months ahead. But it was worth the sacrifice of my sleep, every minute of it, for the sake of his children. And finally a close monitoring paid off at the exuberant end of the fifth month. He started to regain harmonious feelings and slowly stepped out of the darkness.

In a sense, I felt more relieved than he did. I couldn't bear the idea of being answerable to his fate had it been for my inaction to properly provide help.

By the end of the following winter, he ran into an old friend of his from childhood at a school reunion and talked her into getting to know me. He did not intuit my unlikely answer, however. I respectfully declined and excused myself saying no more. Eventually, the curmudgeon was furious. In me, he saw a man who seemed to have everything but Love. If only he knew.

"Sometimes coincidental events lead to something purposeful, something meant to happen for a greater cause," he insisted and harassed me for a couple of weeks to make the call.

Chapter 14

Air

By any measure, the great depression in a man's life is an unwarranted emptiness. That thought has haunted me for the last couple of days now. This came after a sudden attack of consciousness from years of living in perpetual darkness. My life had not exactly augured as planned, but still I refused to give hope where there was none.

Another sluggish day of interminable meetings and pushing papers came to a much-awaited halt. Every aspect of my being was drained, and more so the mental.

Above all things, I dreaded traveling most. After a hundred times on these familiar ever-lengthening stretches of asphalt, the panoramic sceneries had lost their charm. When I started this job as an insurance investigator, being constantly on the road gave me a sense of liberty, which was what drew me to this career in the first place.

Now I realized that I have been a captive of my own device. Too much of something is never good, a friend had cautioned me once. Or was it a quote from an old Chinese movie? One of those in which the English dubbing is so poorly edited that the speech would end way ahead of the character's lip movements.

On the way back to the hotel, I observed moving spots across the setting sun. They soon materialized into a flock of vociferous migrating geese. Their homeward flight denoted the dawn of spring. A relief. The cold had overstayed its welcome even to a winter enthusiast as I.

As I approached the city limit of Carmel, the flamboyant rays of daylight slowly dissipated into a fluorescent sunset before relaying nature's course onto the obscure of the evening. That divine marvel was the best part of the day. Only the low bit-rate emission of sound waves from the radio grounded me to earth.

After a long, hot shower, I found myself alone again in the unlit square room. As always the silver screen of the television set was my only source of companionship, and also the sole illumination. Feet up, a beer in hand, I savored a well-deserved moment of respite.

On the cable networks, the media broadcast murders, robberies and more debaucheries. My eyes became heavy. A nap seemed to be in place—in those days I rarely slept through an entire night anymore—when out of nowhere a wrinkled piece of paper sticking out from my planner on the lamp table magnetized my attention. It did not take long until I succumbed to curiosity. I found a name and a telephone number penned on it. After a moment of probing my mind, I recalled having written down that information a few weeks earlier.

At the time, it appeared to be of no importance.

My good old friend Don had provided it two weeks ago with great expectations. At his urging, I was to make contact and hopefully develop a promising liaison with that person whom he referred to as *Juliet*. To that, I had responded, "Romeo died a young fella, if you recall."

He dismissed my retort with a "Shut-up, will you?" and claimed that seeing me lonely depressed him with contagious malaise. "No one should live or die alone," he lectured me ad nauseam.

No matter the depth of our friendship, I could never fully get used to the arrogance of that man. As if he knew my philosophy of life. No one knew that much—this castle, with ocean-sized moat and sky-high fortress, was impenetrable.

You've got to love a man who thinks he knows you better than you would yourself. What can I say? That's Don! My brother-in-arms. Those thoughts prompted a smile, one of those things that rarely occurred anymore amid my vapid lifestyle.

I politely declined the offer, thinking that it was inappropriate to call a total stranger. Being brought up old-fashioned was my point of contention. The other truth, which was also the more likely reason, I suspected a jape to get a good laugh at my expense. Don had a propensity for buffoonery. I had not forgotten those early years into our friendship.

The case was sealed and swept under the rug, so it seemed.

Besides, I had had my fair share with the meaningless flings. And so, I had permanently dismissed the notion of companionship without any real merit. Morally converted, I'd much rather be alone and wait for the real deal to come around.

This gave me strength to bear life as it was.

Wide awake now, I diverted my attention to a movie, *What Dreams May Come* if my memory doesn't fail me, while sipping my loneliness away. Another five minutes, or maybe fifteen, went by and still my eyes remained fixed on that insignificant piece of paper. For some reason, I was drawn to it.

I grabbed the note, but, quickly discouraged, slouched back on the lonely cold bed. *Who are you kidding? Nobody stays home on a Friday night but you, loser,* I thought. The chance of catching her would be slim to none.

With each minute that passed by, my resistance gradually abandoned its post until temptation wrestled me down to a tap out. I was bound to make that fateful phone call.

Swiftly, before I changed my mind, I dialed the number.

Somehow I had wished that this courtesy call would get Don out of my hair once and for all. I also made the effort to feel alive again, only if for a little while.

To my surprise a silky-spoken young woman responded after a few rings.

After introducing myself, I told her. “I would like to apologize for intruding upon you, but our friend Don was very persistent that I contact you.”

She giggled.

I had not the slightest clue.

“You mean to tell me that you had no intention of calling me if it wasn’t for your friend?” she replied with a sarcastic tone.

A pause.

I should have never made that call. Now, she had me feel like the insensitive prick that I had become—a lonely-deserving soul.

“Well—”

She interrupted me and carried on. “It’s a relief knowing that I had not been desperately waiting for your call.” She laughed and was about to excuse herself for the night when the gentleman in me finally appeared.

“Wait, please.”

There was something about her. I knew that I was in

trouble at that precise moment. That strong personality of hers was an attribute I couldn't ignore. I engaged her in a conversation, about the weather, anything at all while trying to remain relevant, just to hear that soothing voice.

The most painful and enduring fifteen minutes of my entire life, it seemed.

What do I have to lose? I thought.

From that short exchange, the decibels of sound from her voice undulated through my veins and revitalized my dormant heart.

"You are well-spoken and fit all the descriptions that Don had made of you," she said. "Every bit of it. Now, let me ask you this, if it's not too personal of course. How is that a person such as yourself is still available?"

"It's entirely by choice. To love is to be true to oneself. I am afraid I have not truly explored that side of mine yet."

"Who speaks like that anymore?" She giggled again. "I must say, you are quite a character mister. Awkward, but interestingly different."

Then out of nowhere and also inspired by an old belief that the language of love should only be sung, I started to sing a French song without warning her. Out of nervousness, or fear, perhaps, from spewing more nonsense.

By the end of the song, there was no noise on the other end of the receiver.

It felt as if I had doubled-down on my stupidity.

"I am sorry. I did not mean to make you feel uncomfortable. Some other time perhaps, milady."

"Encore," she said softly.

Suddenly my whole being was lifted high, as carried away by a waft of air in a September morning. Each and every one of her infectious giggles aroused the limbic region of my brain as though the pheromones had made their way through the air waves.

Her voice could have turned the beastliest of men into heavenly docile creatures. I couldn't still entirely fathom what was happening. With such voice, the sounds of words were music to my soul. From those first few minutes into the dialogue, I was mesmerized as lured by the chanting of Sirens to a fatal plunge into the depths of the Seven Seas.

Harmonically-minded after the first hour, we engaged in spirited discussions until dawn, unwilling to let go of the receptors as two hormone-raging teenagers caught in the vortex of love. The painful life stories and the sufferings that we had both endured drew us close. Over the course of that night, we developed a natural bond as if bestowed by the winged-matchmaker himself.

Don was absolutely astounded by our overnight connection and inquired of the recipe to my aphrodisiac. "Genuinely caring for her emotions contributed to a pleasant result," I simply answered.

To little surprise, he did not take me seriously. His *modus operandi* on these matters differed with mine in great disparity. He had a penchant for pick-up lines and embellishing facts about himself. In our youth, I had often accused him of being a spurious imitation of Casanova—the sort of things myths are made of.

Her name was Aline, foreshortened to Ali for popular usage.

In comparison, our compatibility resided with our common knowledge of suffering in the name of love, both lives with no shortage of crisis. From thereon, the emptiness in us filled considerably for what started as a friendship flourished into something much more potent, driven by our mutual *faiblesse* for romanticism.

Upon that first night, Ali had been straightforward about her inability to conceive children.

"If you cannot accept that fact, we should not start anything that will definitely turn sour someday," she insisted. Her tone of voice was always sad at any mention of it. But given the stakes, it was essential the issue be addressed.

"I've been waiting for someone to help me raise my daughter," I said, reassuring her that her infertility was not a cause of concern to me. "Do you happen to know a candidate?"

We spent every night on the phone, losing willfully all senses of reality. It was the chocolate sort of craving that we felt for one another. To make matters more real and interesting, we decided not to share pictures. She had wished to get to know me from the inside first. It worked out for the better on my end. I needed to shed a few pounds.

Two months and twenty-something pounds later, I was on a flight bound to Minnesota. I had volunteered to take on a case, for half the pay, that was in the vicinity of Duluth where she resided.

Moments before our first meeting at MSP airport, I was restless with impatience oozing out of each pore of my body, unsure of how to approach her. In the end, I resolved to overcome my frustration with a hug. The most unnerving thing was perhaps to convince her that I would still be interesting once she unveiled the man behind the receptor.

My winsome charm suddenly disappeared along with my confidence. Drenching sweat, body odor, and discomfort, not to forget that I had left my tongue in the overhead compartment. That was not the kind of indelible impression I had wished to leave upon our first meeting.

And there she was, standing in front of me. A smile-to-die-for on her flawless face, she was wearing a three-piece ensemble that caressed her hourglass figure with elegance. Her highlighted hair was perfectly layered right above her chest which provoked impure thoughts. It did not help the situation at all.

I was wearing my boots to appear taller, and slimmer.

That first glance at her left me with yearning adolescent eyes. Her impeccable looks and personality, gifts from above, were in perfect harmony. I stared awkwardly long at her face unable to move my eyes from it. Famished for those lips, I thought about kissing them if only it would have been appropriate.

God did not create all women equally. She was, in every prismatic aspect, the incarnation of *la Femme Idéale*. My sincere apology to anyone who should be offended by this brute remark. Truly.

This was the moment I had been waiting for all these years, or should I say my whole life.

That feeling of complete ecstasy was one I would never forget. Yet ironically, it had been so long, I had forgotten how it felt to be alive again.

It was beyond me to have been blessed with such a beautiful face to match that soothing voice. She was the conduit to happiness, the kind of woman I would follow the length of my days.

As we hugged in the center of the baggage claim area, a man dressed in a gray trench coat winked at me with his right thumb up. "This would be a good time to genuflect."

A bit perplexed, I responded, "Pardon?"

"Have you forgotten the ring?" he asked me before turning his gaze in Ali's direction.

"Things will come along in due time, I'm sure," I slightly blushed and answered while looking profoundly inside her bottomless eyes.

Now she was blushing with twice the shade of rouge on me.

"Well, young man, you need to make haste. She's a keeper," he replied while his wife, I supposed, joined him with their luggage. They soon left but not before the man managed to give me discreetly a tap on the shoulder as to say, *you lucky man!*

We spent the entire weekend without losing sight of each other. At her request, I extended my stay for another week, which spared me the humiliation of begging had she not. And I would have, with no hesitation.

Before long, she secretly smuggled love into my life until a feeling of completeness filled the void inside. The world was a wonderful place again. My love for her was inexplicable yet real. I was madly in love with her.

I no longer knew any other way to love.

My life had changed overnight. The combined strength and softness of that woman had blessed me with infinite regalement. My prayers for a better life had been answered and my world no longer reflected the sorrow of past. She held that electrifying power in the palm of her hands and unleashed it to silence my demons at will, time after time.

All my torments vanished within the forbearance that she devoted to me as our love culminated to higher ground. At that point, everything seemed aligned with the stars, distance being the last obstacle.

After a year of paradise on earth and half a dozen

more visits, we were engaged. There was an element of complicity which constituted the foundation of our love in that first year. She was one end of the rope tied to the beauty of life, I was the other end tied to passion, and together we formed a knot.

She moved in with me the following spring.

In the mornings, when my eyelids were still closed, she would spend long moments staring at me and softly retrace the contour of my face with the tip of her index finger. While quietly humming a tune, she'd kiss the back of my neck sending shivers down my spine to bring me back from the deep slumber.

I had not slept like a cub in years.

Every day I could hardly wait to come home to her warm embrace. On her end, she felt truly lucky to have found her best friend in me, and she would always whisper her elation to my soul before her lips were introduced to mine all over again.

In silent agreement, we entered our *Bubble of Happiness*.

Chapter 15

The Indian Summer

She left.

One evening, after a few days on the road, I came home to find the house unlit and the gravel drive empty. More devastated than confounded, I knew right away that something was out of place. I had not been able to reach her the whole day. It was the kind of feeling that wrenches your inside in knots and leaves your lungs begging for oxygen.

The *Dear John* on the dresser read that she needed time away to reflect on the ongoing genocide of our emotions. She was exhausted from the reviled arguments and the chaos in our life. By that, she meant my stubbornness and my unwillingness to open up.

Well into the second year of our relationship and by then the end of the honey moon phase as to most relationships, things started to change right under the nose of my conscience.

For some time now, we'd been having issues, but I wasn't aware that the severity of the situation had reached the boiling point. The incisions of emotional wounds that we had inflicted upon one another, whether consciously or intentionally or not, revealed to be more punitive to our relationship.

Our love had fallen from grace amid this ineluctable madness. But it wasn't until our thoughts ceased to be in concert that her resolve to leave had cemented.

In a vision, dated as far as the birth of her emptiness, she had waited for her soul mate by the waterfalls and had recognized in me the face of that mystical person when she first laid eyes on me—she often reminded me in our quiet moments. Love gave us such invincibility that failing was never in the forecast.

Yet she had gone back to Duluth.

I was left alone to collect the pieces of our shattered dream. I had been awarded yet another situation on my plate. For the next three weeks, I stayed at a squalid motel. The very sight of our empty home was too much of a strain to confront.

My world had crumbled apart, and along with it our life.

A life that had freed our souls from loneliness.

A life engineered to our perfection but did not produce the result desired.

That summer I was back at square one. Alone. The void inside re-opened, and it funneled all happiness out of me. Night and day became one.

I was pained. I stopped eating. I stopped sleeping. I stopped dreaming. But I could not stop hurting from what meager remained of our love. Try as I could, I was incapable of finding immunity from the impact of her sudden disappearance.

In the wildest of my deliriums, I had never imagined that the darkness would be present in my life again. How did we get here? I pondered and pondered under a disappearing flutter of hope.

From the very beginning, she had sensed my torments, and at the exclusion of her own, she was determined to help me cope with my distress. As if destined from birth for this responsibility she would not renounce on her objective, a toil so grueling I would always be indebted to her.

In her, I saw a younger version of Maman.

Despite her efforts, I refrained from sharing certain aspects of my past. It wasn't so much that I was reluctant to open up, but more so about being selective of what I revealed. It could be a natural instinct or a defense mechanism, but I had struggled my whole life with letting people in.

Our fall, however, started when I bought a home as a

testament of my love for her. She did not see it that way. To her, it represented an unnecessary burden, a prelude to disaster. She had expressed concern that we could not afford it because she was still pursuing her nursing degree and not working. But I reassured her that I was capable of handling the bills on my own.

Driven by the White-Picket-Fence dream, I submerged myself with more work at the expense of our quality time. Things deteriorated even further from there as we slowly departed from the script of our life. We had wished for the same things although with very different approaches to achieving them.

Our love never recovered. Even worse, setbacks kept piling up.

In the following month, I was slapped with a child-custody suit. After so many years, Mona decided to get full custody of Iris. I was in disbelief. She must have sensed my happiness and tried to sabotage it. The case quickly depleted my bank account all the while combusting the last remaining enclave of my mental fortitude.

She could have not chosen a better time.

Between my busy work schedule and the court dates back and forth to Santa Barbara, I did not have much room left for Ali. My serenades turned into silence while the reflection of her splendor faded into the obscure of depression. The months went by, and her patience bled into frustration as she became more exigent of my time. She excoriated me that she had signed up to embrace eternity with me and certainly not to be left in the grip of loneliness again.

Very soon the situation swerved out of control. With a different event looming in the horizon each day, we slowly detached from our sacred bond. Our *Modus Vivendi* was subjected to a complete makeover. Neither of us liked that change, but neither was willing to compromise.

It became almost impossible to communicate anymore.

By my failures to read her frustrations, I had only perpetuated this tense situation. Her vexation blew into erupted ire with so little warning that it left my guard entirely decentralized. This was something new. For the first of several times to come, I witnessed that side of her never seen before.

As our relationship slalomed down the slippery slopes of Mt. Failure, I began to make every effort to condense the empty space between us by outlining the measures we needed to adopt if our love was to be spared. For that, I needed to go back to the intrinsic ancestry of her anguish.

The only child, Ali was orphaned at early age and was raised by her grandmother. She had felt alone most of her life, an emptiness of far greater depth than mine. Too caught up with everything else, I had not realized soon enough that she was wearing her own chains.

She was fighting a greater war than I could never fully understand. Everyone comes with some darkness. Ali was no different.

She had hoped to restore her life in pleasure in order to smother the pain. And I did not deliver. Contrary to my initial intention, I added to her distress.

Along with the seasons, frustrations settled in our minds as D-Day bunkers destabilizing all communication routes with mental barricades. Disputes lurched into festering feuds for we could not find within ourselves to draw an armistice line. Between times, our efforts at *détente* were recurrently broadsided by the easily-provoked arguments. In this case, silence did not mean peace. It was concealed frustration still brewing in the back burner.

In great desperation, I waved the flag of surrender because of the ongoing custody case. Time passed, lots of things happened, but none divulged any indication in favor of a reconciliation. We were worlds apart from compromise.

Increasingly, I realized that we had lost our ways to fend for an irreversible catastrophe, not so much because of our lack of communication, but mostly because of our failure to engage on issues of importance. If anyone expected the story to end with a happily ever after, that person was only me. In any event, I never let myself doubt the best in others, and I was not about to begin, especially with her.

Perhaps I should have done more.

I should have listened to her cries for help.

I reached out, a little too late perhaps, but I tried.

For any consolation, if that should apply, I was not the only aggrieved party to feel the ravage of separation. Back home with Grandma, Ali whiled her days in desolation and made no efforts to conceal her anguish when calling me. She longed for the nights spent in my arms and was depressed as much as I was, if not more.

She had hoped that time apart would bring us closer. A test of strength, she said.

I did not share her optimism. I was not afforded a choice in this trial of separation in the first place. It was mandated to me.

She had once told me, "My darling, without the anger, we are perfect for each other."

I partially agreed, my only contention being that we seemed to live in perpetual anger. It's a real tragedy when two people truly love each other but cannot work out their differences.

The mixture of our frustrations mired in a doomed love affair. Yet, somewhere in the cosmos of our love, the flame was still burning. She was gone, but her heart had remained with me, bolted as the center of gravity to our world.

One morning, I was driving, from ward to ward, to an unknown destination for the sake of escaping, with only her in my thoughts and the fresh air as my voice of reason.

Uncertain of what the future would bring, my heart was racing fast.

After so much happiness, it was twice as hard to get used to doing things and going places alone again. I did not know how to unwind anymore. It was the kind of loneliness that could kill the unprepared mind. Once you catch a glimpse of the light, the darkness is even scarier than before because you have actually tasted firsthand what it feels like to be loved.

This new darkness seemed to have a stronger hold on me. It became more powerful, even arrogant, knowing that I came back to it. It whispered to me: *The door is wide open, go as you please, but this is where you belong.*

In the end, all roads led me back to our home. I stopped there for a moment to savor the happiness of a past life. Memories of her were never too far from my mind. I imagined her standing by the door, waiting for me. Coming home to her was the best part of the day, impatient as always to see her beautiful smile that had illuminated my whole world ever since.

With my face pushed against the window screen, the chanting of my heart turned into languid beats. I lingered for her caress and found no deliverance from loneliness. In the center of my misery, faith was all I had left in my possession to keep my head above water.

In that incongruous moment, I took courage at hand and unlocked the main door. Inside the house, the air was redolent of the sillage of her perfumes and unfettered more sorrow within. I resented the implication that she left so unceremoniously. As hard as it was then to just formulate of such eventuality, a consequence too frightening to even contemplate, now it had become a reality.

I drove off.

Meanwhile, I needed to remain strong for my daughter's case. Head hung low, I was sapped to the point of insanity. The legal fees had left me financially hard-pressed.

In the scramble of the situation, I was confiding in Don, but I detected a profusion of indifference settling in the tone of his voice, as if he could be at no further assistance. There was a questionable sentiment of distance coming from him that left me mystified.

I was disheartened by the lukewarm support he extended.

Chapter 16

Rain on Me

Along the melancholy that stretched into the length of each day, surfs of chagrin splashed incessantly against the corroded façades of our bleeding hearts. Once again, loneliness reigned repressively in our world while distance inflicted ubiquitous torments to our souls through each spasm of internal panic.

By then, we lived separate lives and longed for each other's company to unrestrained boundaries of our unflagging love. On my end, the flow of life almost came to a halt, but I managed.

Distance spares no one.

Consistent with old habits, we spent every night conversing until we trekked into a mournful sleep allowing the climax of the day to attenuate, but it was evident that the meretricious comfort of our voices became a nuisance more than anything else. In dreams, our souls evaded the ugly vignette of reality—only then we found peace as our hearts stopped churning momentarily from the pain of being apart.

"My love, we could've had it all. I don't understand how something so beautiful can be this painful," she sobbed. "I just don't know how to go about this loneliness anymore."

"Only time will tell." I replied.

"What if time would only set us apart farther?"

Answers, pleasant few I offered. "That was the risk you were willing to take." I said, almost indifferent, with a cathedral-size ego showing in the tone of my voice.

"Don't you see that I only left so that we may appreciate each other better?" she fired back.

"There it goes again. That's us, right? Two minutes of peace and the rest of the time is hell," I said. "Why not just let it be? At least, we'll have a real reason to hurt. Don't you think so?"

"No. This will not, and should not, end like this. We worked too hard to end like this."

A much-needed pause. I was still not breathing. I regrouped and found peace again within the tone of my voice. "What do you suggest we do then?" I asked.

"Come to me. I want to be with you. I miss your

scent, everything, even the senseless arguments," she said, while sobbing harder by the moment.

As the demoralizing effects of separation elevated into mounds of frustrations, we finally came to an accord and made plans to reunite. *This cannot be the end*, I couldn't agree more. After all we've been through.

With haste, I led an amorous expedition to one of the northernmost cold ends of the land to restore harmony in our hearts.

When she first saw me again outside her grandma's snow-covered driveway, there was a glycerin moment in her eyes. We held for a long moment, speechless, letting our emotions speak the words we couldn't muster out. We were alive again with total neglect of time and space, and everything else.

Our love so intense only the pain could equal. And that was the scary part.

In the three months since we'd last seen each other, Ali had lost one dress size but remained beautiful as ever, if not more. Depression had had an adverse effect on her in that regard. Not so much for me.

She held my hands and cried.

Inside the house, Grandma was patiently waiting. She had prepared a feast for me, and I felt like I should never leave this place again. I could get used to this kind of life.

Both of my grandmothers had passed several years before, and it made me appreciate her even more. To have this matriarchal figure this late into my life again was nothing short of bliss.

We spent the rest of the week in a Scandinavian-styled cabin at the beachfront shoreline of Lake Superior, catching up on what we'd missed from being apart and trying to mend what was broken. A freak freeze had shut down the docks for weeks to come and rendered the place almost deserted.

Everything was peaceful, something we desperately needed.

A week went by in the space of a blink. As always time seemed to elapse faster in happier moments. Given the circumstances, we knew all too well that when I returned to California, the pain, rising *en masse*, would resurface, turning each day into a non-stop roller coaster ride of depression.

Alas, that evening came the inevitable moment we both feared—the infamous farewells. Ali was leaning against the door, next to the unmade bed, wearing nothing but a silky see-through burgundy peignoir, her favorite color. Hiding her emotions, she focused on projections of naked branches waltzing on the adjacent wall that served as a modest theatrical screen.

In devastating silence, I was packing my luggage.

She strained to maintain her composure by clenching her tiny fists to harness courage, but she had not fooled me. Never before either. I felt the same way, bone-tough on the outside and marrow-soft in the inside, yet a much accredited impostor than she was in the mastery of contrivance.

Pestered, we were both bombarded by devastation, knowing that it would be long before our next reunion. Our hearts melted away despite the bitter cold that left us powerless against the wickedness of life.

As I carried the last of my valises to the rental under the gloomy starless canopy, the vibrant whistling of the gales kept my mind immersed in ambivalent thoughts, bifurcated in between leaving or staying a while longer. But there was no use to complicate the situation when so little time remained.

My whole body became frigid from the wintry air, or perhaps from a deep feeling of sorrow inside. Regardless of the source, I was numb from heart to soul. I could not feel anymore the chilling air and the snowflakes that blanketed my heavy navy pea coat.

Careful in her steps, Ali came out to send me off, her hair pulled-up in a messy chignon. Translucent streaks from her forlorn eyes trickled down her face and turned into pebbles of crystal as they came in contact with the gelid ground.

Her eyes implored me to stay but the words would not come out.

She knew better. I had to leave. There was no alternative.

Then abruptly, she cried out loud and carelessly. Her cries reached across the cold black fabric of night and drew out concerned neighbors. She held tightly onto my waist and abandoned herself in the warmth of my arms. I stared long into her dreary eyes and devoured her lips a last time.

"I will come back for you. You know I will. As soon as this case is settled."

To make matters worse, the snowflakes stopped falling, and the dark rain took succession in a downpour of sleet as it always had whenever my life was in the keep of grief. Time after time, the omnipresent rain had reflected on my sorrow—although this time it wasn't the same kind of soothing rain found in Seattle.

Abhorrent was the situation at the least. It unfolded in my mind as those black-and-white films with a dispirited ending accompanied by a solo violin melody that accentuated the tragedy of the moment, while the chyron appeared in the center of the screen with the word *Fin*.

We remained immobile for a segment of the clock before I slowly detached from her, desperately fighting off my emotions not to succumb to the anguish of departing.

With a goliath frog in my throat, I drove off, leaving Ali in agonizing cries. As I slowly sped away, I perceived through the rear-view mirror the reflection of her beautiful face gleaming under the lamppost. Bit by bit, the receding image of her paleness blurred away until it blended with the colors of the night, and finally into visual dissipation.

Long after she was out of sight, her cries kept tolling heavily in my head. I started missing her even more with all the might of what was left of my battered strength. Alone in my thoughts, I kept on driving in the middle of the night under the raging precipitation and sharp pellets of ice—the dagger plunged in deeper.

After a newly crescent moon, I came back to a ghost town. I was broken inside but showed resilience in order to hide my sorrow, maybe due pride—another great sin of mine. In the lonely corner of her world, Ali cried herself to sleep every single night since my departure.

Every morning, an onslaught of nostalgia disrupted the peace within while my head spun into a disoriented whirl. In remedy, my wanderlust often escaped far and away to the winter scenery of a harmonious repose extracted from a picturesque depiction of the Alps Chain. The memories of the beautiful highlands of Switzerland always brought me so much closer to the edge of Heaven. I had fallen in love with that nonpareil place ages ago when traveling across Europe. What a wonderful treat to the soul. I gasped silently inside, lost in a vague distraction of mind.

I felt relieved, content even, for an insipid instant.

Sitting on the foot of my four-poster bed, I remained contemplative while exploring the sudden vastness of my room. As always, her smile occupied each slit of my thoughts and caused my sleep unattainable.

My entire being, heart, mind and soul, was still exhausted from the trip back home. Everything was blank and meaningless. Curled in a ball, I kept my eyes fixated on the wall while a wave of lethargy washed over me.

I shut the blinds in desperate hope to retreat in dream or enchantment, whichever might've come first. All I found was darkness, no comfort, just a feeling of desolation. The emptiness gained momentum, but somehow I had gotten used to it over the years, so it bothered me none, or perhaps should I say less.

To most men, it would have been hard to absorb let alone survive the pain inside. But not to me. Not to this old heart of mine, encrusted and hardened by deceptions. Well, so I felt at the moment without putting much thought into it to validate the truth.

Ultimately, I surrendered to my emotions. I was powerless against my loneliness, once again. Cold sweats permeated through my night robe. I was submerged in a swamp of uncertainty impossible to circumnavigate about.

Alone, I was mummified by lamentation as the world around exhaled steams of despair in my life, again. Having never been subjected to this kind of pain before, I had no idea on how to process this feeling and just wanted to scream—and breathe fire.

I had left my heart and soul in Duluth.

All through the compilation of weeks that finally extended into February the same routine flavored our lives. But, in an inconceivable twist, when I called her one evening, the tone of her voice changed, unpredictably as the vagaries of the sky. Her anger soared above the ozone layer, and I was clueless about this sudden change of her state of mind. The same squabbles and arguments recurred, and the same scenario unfolded.

"Is there something I should know?" I asked.

No immediate answer. Then suddenly she voiced her frustration, "I really don't want this back-and-forth between us anymore. It's beyond me."

"What's going on?" I pressed for more answers. "Why are you acting so different tonight?

It was the same old dance all over again.

"I don't want to talk about it right now. In fact, I don't want to talk to you at all, and anymore!" Her voice elevated, and then she went silent.

I was no stranger to those mood swings. Nonetheless the reason remained a mystery.

At that point, all hope perished within the never-ending altercations. It seemed for a brief moment, an instant of solace, that our love was getting better but reality showed that we could not find truce in our hearts.

In a brief statement, she said that she had reached the point where "enough is enough" and wished for me to get out of her life forever. Without further explanations she cut off the engagement.

I was faced with the certainty of having lost my best friend.

Crestfallen and emotionally eviscerated, I complied and sent her a Farewell note:

Ma Chère Ali,

I wish things could have been different between "You & Me" so Grandma would always be present every day in my life—alongside you. Sorry if I could not give you the life you have wished for, inside our bubble.

Adieu,

Tristan

Chapter 17

Schadenfreude

Time lingered in suspension between the spaces of the falling grains of sand and took all the joy that we had built together, even the littlest things that once made our days agreeable—breakfast in bed, catching a late night movie, or shopping for trainers though we never jogged.

Now they all reflected nothing but *tristesse*.

If my faith in love was squashed, nothing had renewed it. The atmosphere carried no ambition for better days ahead. In a way, it did reconcile me back to reality from the emotional disturbances that had been pouring all over me for unmeasured time now.

All seemed calm on the surface from the self-imposed submission to what I couldn't change until one lonesome night

I received a call from Ali. She had wished to hear my voice, once more, to pacify the distress of her soul. "I miss your serenades and your touch," she said. "It's harder than I could have ever imagined."

I was not in the least surprised. I was in no better shape myself.

"My love, I am truly sorry for the pain I've caused you. I made a terrible mistake out of anger, and I hope that you can find it in your heart to forgive me someday," she said.

I didn't say much and just listened, half-asleep and dizzy from the vodka.

Unable to let go, she couldn't live with herself any longer should the truth be exposed. She'd had a host of reserved thoughts never before addressed to my attention, which she had initially intended to take to the grave, but now incurred in guilt, she had committed herself to a tell-all. She advised me, in a trembling voice, that the details would be painful. Her voice congealed from hesitation for an instant, before giving me the essential piece of evidence:

Don.

As soon as his name was brought up, I was wide awake—and sober.

After a considerable silence, she explained that Don

had warned her that I have had a change of heart about marrying her because I could not accept her infertility after all—this was the reason that made her leave.

He also told her that I have been seeing an old flame behind her back which explained my frequent absences. This was the last drop that made her break off the engagement.

Don, being my best friend and my only confidant, it did not take much convincing for her to believe. He had seen an opening and acted upon it in her moments of weakness. To my stupefaction, he had added many more awful fabrications.

As expected, she believed every single word without giving me the benefit of the doubt. In her bewilderment, she fell prey to his Machiavellian mind tricks.

Then swelled in blind fury she axed our love into shreds.

Granted, she was already very close to the edge, but ultimately, Don had sent her completely over it. Her reaction was so quick that she never considered the consequences against accusations that should have been challenged and refuted. And the extreme measures she had taken against me had tarnished our relationship forever.

She also confessed that, after our break-up, Don started to come around more often to give her comfort—the coup had bolstered his confidence, she claimed. But all things came to an end one evening.

Don could never hold his liquor and while intoxicated he finally blurted out his whole master plan. That night, she fell apart when she discovered that he had lied to her about everything and she found the courage to call me. She might've been coerced into his sordid schemes at a moment of upheaval in her life, but things would never be the same between us anymore. It was much more than a case of guilty by association. She'd broken our trust—the most important ingredient in a relationship, I was told.

In a world gone insane, she took cognizance of the grave fault of her deeds and begged for forgiveness, "My love, we were both betrayed by Don."

Abruptly, her silky Siren voice had stopped having effect on me. "No, I have been betrayed by both him and you!" I replied firmly. "Whatever reasons you may give me won't change the fact that you chose to believe him and abandoned me when I most needed you. Have a good life!" I told her and slammed the phone.

There was no turning back. Our relationship was truly over this time.

Everything reverted back to my original instinct taken from Don's indifference and his louche behavior when I needed his support. I had sensed his foul purpose some time ago yet with no absolute certainty. From being the person of interest, he'd become the prime suspect.

My mind lunged ahead for answers. Things started to make sense. Deep inside, I wished that my good old friend had nothing to do with the dissolution of my life, but I couldn't deny my intuition anymore. I had known Don to exaggerate facts and lie, which made her accusations absolutely plausible.

My thoughts were scattered in all places.

What could have driven this man to madness?

Why?

No answers.

In the predawn darkness of the next day, I decided to confront him. Out of moral obligation, I had to afford him the same assumption of innocence that I had reproached Ali for not giving me.

After two failed attempts, he finally returned my calls.

"I thought we agreed to stay away from each other's business!" were my first words to him as soon as I answered.

Barely awakened, he replied, "What are you talking about? I hope you know that it's only five-fifteen a.m."

"Don't flash your ignorance credentials at me! You know what I'm talking about," I added. "Why did you tell her such lies?"

"I don't know what you're talking about! Are you feeling okay, bro?"

"Don't bro me! You know well what I'm talking about! You can't fool me twice!" I insisted.

"Elaborate dude. I have no clue—Ahaaaah—Are you making drunken arguments again?" he asserted with an impassive yawn.

Immediately, I brought forth the allegations issued against him.

Guilty beyond reasonable doubt, he knew that his scheme was no longer a matter of secrecy, but still he tried to disprove my initial suspicions. Caught in a swarm of lies, he groped for an answer then spluttered a *purée* of justifications and pointed everything back at Ali. “I know that you spoke to her but—uh—you have to trust me, my hands are clean from any foul play—and uh—she is trying to break our friendship,” he stammered further.

This was certainly a bad case of foot-in-mouth.

“And why would she do that?” I replied.

“Because she wants to control you and—uh—as long as I stand in the way, she can’t,” he fired back.

His response whirred with annoyance in my head. “Malarkey! That does not sound a bit like her. Tell me the damn truth!”

“She’s obsessed with you and uh, wants you all to herself.”

Those last words sent me into an uncontrollable silly laugh. For a moment I almost wanted to commiserate with that poor soul. “How pathetic are you? You can do better than that, c’mon man! Do you wish to plead the fifth now, or shall we continue?” I asked.

In a last hope in preventing the possibility of anything more, I had to listen to the end just in case he was telling the truth. Besides, that was what I set out to do in the first place. *Nobody can lie all the time*, I thought. Except for somebody like Don who would do anything to win by any means necessary. How could have I forgotten his abundance of characters?

"You have to believe me! She's behind everything! She's wanted to dismantle our friendship for some time now! Trust me!" His voice suddenly carried out the tone of exasperation.

For a minute, he tried to create a false equivalency to alleviate the pressure off of him, but his allegations were widely baseless.

"I don't believe you! She might keep things from me but she doesn't lie—at least not to me. On the other hand, you have deceived and lied to me on numerous occasions! I just ignored that side of yours because I know how immature you can be at times."

Fifteen seconds of dead silence elapsed.

A great deal of tension arose as the discussion went on, which made him think about his words very carefully. Then a thought occurred to me. I realized that I needed to take a different approach on the situation. I bit back my tongue and reshuffled my thoughts to plot my next move. I had always known him for having a quick temper, and the only way to get anything out would be to tap into that spot. And so I meticulously pushed his buttons further.

"Do you remember the day I called you after Ali left?" I asked.

"I'm not sure, but go on. Refresh my mind."

"Of course not. You were nowhere to be found for

two weeks and did not even bother returning my calls."

"So? What's your point?" he replied, unfazed.

"Well, it's because you were hiding from me. Too afraid that you might accidentally incriminate yourself, right? We all know that your big mouth opens for business around the clock," I added. "Who else would know about our dirty laundry? You forgot that single detail, did you? I guess you are not as smart as you make out, Einstein."

Silence.

"Your impeccable instincts have even predicted that an unforeseen event would muddy our relationship. Do you remember that? Or do you need more refreshing?"

Still no reply on his part. A clear indication of a build-up of frustration.

"What's the matter? Cat got your tongue?"

Upon those words, I purposely laughed with condescension. I've learned well—all those years being bullied by Hercules had finally paid off.

Incurably criminal, he knew at that point, that there was no use protesting his innocence anymore and willingly adopted an air of arrogance as a measure of defiance.

The prospect of gaining a momentum brought me great excitement.

Almost instantaneously, the devil inside appeared. With that window of opportunity wide open, it was just a matter of time before the truth came out.

"You got nothing on me, dude," he said in a mocking tone.

I did not mince words in my rebuttal. "On the contrary. I know how devious you can be. I just never thought that you would unleash your evil on me someday. I've had bad vibes about you ever since the day she broke off the engagement. Something was telling me that you have everything to do with it!"

"You're damn right, moron! Can you stomach it? You deserve every ounce of the pain!" He barked into the receptor in a brutal voice.

Almost brought to tears, I sighed in silent disbelief. "Why? I have always been good to you. I loved you like a brother. Why?" I asked him over and again.

"Because of you, my life is just a big joke. How does it feel to lose everything?"

"You should be institutionalized! What have I done to you? Tell me!"

"You took everything from me!"

"What did I take from you?"

"You stole her away from the beginning and ruined my life!"

Puzzled, I was taken aback for a moment. "You mean your ex-wife?"

"Yes. Who else? You took away the only person that I truly love!"

"Haven't we gone through this before?" I asked with frustration.

All these years, I thought that we had set aside that incident once and for all. I was wrong. This new revelation left me more shocked than upset.

"You know that I've always been loyal to you to a fault, and that I have never disrespected you in any way. So how am I guilty of anything?" I asked again.

To which he responded, "Things have never been the same ever since she met you!"

"And that's the reason why I told you to stay away from her. But you couldn't and wouldn't. So assume the responsibilities! I have never wronged you. You know that much!"

He knew that I was speaking the truth and remained silent for a moment trying to find the right words for a pitiful come back. I did not give him such chance.

"So why did you introduce me to Ali? Why did you hound me down for weeks to call her?" I asked angrily.

Instead of asking for absolution to be forgiven, he resolved on projecting his own internal pain with a response slathered in sarcasm and hurtful insults. "What do you think, Sherlock? Ali was my friend before she knew you, so it did not take much to manipulate her. The rest was just a game of patience. It's what you call a Double Whammy. Check Mate, loser!" It was a gargantuan exclamation point at the end of that provocative statement.

Don was known to bloviate at great length, but when need be, he also knew how to use the fewest possible words to cause the most damage, leaving everything in shambles in his path. And at this he excelled. A natural, his unmatched talent in that line was unparalleled.

"I wanted you to have my life and feel the pain of losing everything," he shouted out while laughing maniacally.

In typical fashion, his behavior was not out of character. The lack of moral fiber in his persona was still hard to digest. He had reached new depths that no light had ever been before.

This was when I laid to rest the grace of my tongue and spoke in plain jargon. "You douchebag! You waited for the right moment when our relationship was at its most fragile stage to put the final nail in the coffin. Go to hell, carpetbagger!" I shouted back at him on the top of my lungs.

It was a good thing that we were not in a face-à-face situation, our disagreement would have been dragged into the spotlight for public consumption. It would be quite a spectacle if that were to be the case.

Things could have been so much worse, indeed.

"Well, surely a self-serving man like you who took everything from me would not begrudge me a little revenge. I guess now we are even, aren't we? And there's nothing you can do about it, jackass. Your relationship with her is damaged beyond repair," he asserted with depraved indifference.

In the space of a thought, I chose not to dignify his deranged comments with a response. But whether I admitted it or not, he was right. His actions had cost us dearly. Don had been the character being kept hidden in plain sight, the least suspected one, and would only be revealed as significant within the context for effect. The apocalypse theme running deep in his mind, he enjoyed every bit of my downfall.

Deep-seeded in his persona, the laws of morality had never been no more than a suggestion. Target locked-on, finger on the trigger, I was a sitting duck—death by deception.

At the end of the heated exchange, I took a deep breath and as calmly as humanly anyone can be under duress, I said to him, "If you and I were stranded in the middle of the ocean with only one life jacket, I would have chosen to drown without any hesitation. So long, slim!"

Chapter 18

The Salesman

Late one devil-blazing Saturday afternoon, I signed up for a billiard tournament at Malina's Bar & Grill, a favorite hangout spot in downtown. The first prize amounted to peanuts, but it was more for the ladies than anything else that we all crammed in—and the hickory-smoked barbecued short ribs too, to be fair. Over the years, I had become an avid player with an adroit sense of control of the cue ball only rivaled by a lack of focus from alcohol impairment.

The word-of-mouth advertisement and the fliers invited people to come to the tournament. And come they did, in droves. By the time anyone who needed to be there was present, the Western saloon-style cavernous room was packed tight, shoulder-to-shoulder, with barely enough space for the pool sticks to make their way around the tables. The tournament finally started after all the participants had registered their information and paid a small entry fee.

My first opponent was a ridiculously tall man with a mohawk and a saddle nose, whose past glory in the Navy was tattooed along his bulging upper right arm. He was quite a sight, in contrast with me. The locals called him "Blue" due to his tendency to leave bruises on anyone in disagreement with his views, as small as they were, although he was besmirched more for his poor sportsmanship than his hostility.

He seemed the sort no one in their right mind would dare to trifle with. Much of what I heard seemed to be nothing but gossip and rumors up until now. I felt compelled to forfeit the game. The problem, however, was that he could not stand losing, much less to those who resorted in throwing the game.

I was faced with a serious dilemma and had to guard becoming another victim.

Into the middle of the first game in a set of best-two-out-of-three, a shrieking sound rang out. A fight broke out by the bar. Violent screaming, pushing, and shoving ensued. All at once, the laughter was gone. In the full excitement of the moment, amid the *mêlée*, someone threw a beer bottle that landed on the side of a man's head and cracked it open. Things happened quickly, but I seemed to recognize the poor soul whose back was against the floor with his arms raised in desperate supplication.

More out of obligation than eagerness, I rushed over to break up the fight. Thankfully, Blue kept the other three men at bay. That was more commitment than he had ever invested to uphold peace, I was later told. No one understood why. I was just glad he did.

The bloodied man on the floor was none other than Don. With some grunts and groans, he tried to get up. His inimitable sense of style, which was what truly separated him from everyone and also the cause of the affray, had not escaped my mind. We had met some time ago at a banquet at the family farm.

In the past, I'd been knocked off my feet on a few occasions but never for these types of senseless motives. I could not even begin to comprehend the level of pain this man was going through on a daily basis.

Outright scared, he was in all degrees of psychosis. I helped him up and told the owners, whom I knew well, "Don't worry fellas, I'll take him to the ER."

No one bothered calling the cops. The show must go on. Blue parted the waves of people in front of us with his long arms to clear the way toward the exit door. We marched behind as in procession.

Miraculously, I did not have to forfeit after all.

On the way to the hospital, Don swore allegiance to me. This marked the threshold of our friendship.

Things have changed since then.

'I wanted you to have my life and feel the pain of losing everything.'

'I wanted you to have my life and feel the pain of losing everything.'

'I wanted you to have my life and feel the pain of losing everything.'

'I wanted you to have my life and feel the pain of losing everything.'

'I wanted you to have my life and feel the pain of losing everything.'

Don's trenchant words played vigorously over and over inside my head like a song set on auto-play. Abruptly, I saw in my mind the reflection of his face transform into a distinctive image of Mephistopheles. I discerned the tiny horns, the pointy ears, the lifeless dark pupils, the darkened mahogany color of his rugged-skin, and the pronounced smirk that revealed his razor-sharp fangs.

With haze swirling around me, I was transported into a different world, into a different dimension. I had landed in the lair of the Grand Master himself, and I felt the whips of the vivid scarlet blazes scorching my petrified soul. Eminently, the darkness and a malodorous sulfuric stench invaded the space all around. Ominous layers of dark clouds veiled instantly all lifeforms and matters into the eeriness of the night.

In no time, the weather turned vile and shuttled the blows of the wind to my ears into malefic susurrus.

Goose-bumps erected every single hair of my body and the little voice inside, awakened, exhorted tumultuously all my senses.

All the dots were connected.

In the bowels of the circumstances, I remembered my younger brother's heedful warnings that my distorted belief in the goodness of men would cost me dearly someday.

The nerd was darn right.

All doubts set aside, I held Don in contempt for the cataclysm of my world. The once friend who had shared my most intimate joys and insecurities was in fact a fiend with a stratagem intended to inflict pain and sorrow upon me.

I was asphyxiated within my own blind trust in him.

In all of those years, Don had made me believe that evil had no business in our friendship. And I bought into it. Lie after lie, he had deceived me knowing that my loyalty for him would overshadow any suspicions. Not for a single moment had it crossed my mind that he had secretly kept a grudge against me—a grudge that should not have been in the first place which had ultimately turned into hatred.

Such madness would always transcend beyond my understanding.

With my knees deeply-seeded in the muddy ground, I felt diabolic voices ring screeching decibels in my head, leaving the moral compass of my reason disoriented. I was at a point where I could no longer bring myself to gather my wits.

I remained on my knees, head down, as though waiting for decapitation by the guillotine of betrayal. Who would have known that my dear friend was none other than my executioner?

As a wireless marionette, I fell on my back and writhed on the dirt looking into the nebulous sky helplessly as the world around me spun in endless vertigo.

I had been Judased by one of the persons I trusted the most.

I loved that man like a brother. I trusted that man with my life. I trusted that man with my daughter's life. That man whom I had sheltered from despair over and over.

What had this world come to? I pondered, but I had no answers.

Don also had a fissure in his soul, to the difference that I was patching mine with love, he was filling his with hate.

In complete contravention of morality, he had wished for me to share his internal sufferings to find some sort of justice from his own struggles. In his quest to destroy me, he foresaw that Ali was the missing link to my doom. Being the closest person to me, he knew all the critical details and phases of our relationship and fancied that this final blow would finish me off.

And it did.

In a well-orchestrated conspiracy, he had successfully dissolved my relationship with Ali. The sycophant's actions were premeditated and meticulously engineered to ensure a definite victory—an inglorious victory that only a madman would commemorate.

Yet a victory nonetheless.

During our entire friendship, I had helped him unconditionally in all aspects of life, trying to bring him back to the light. For as long as I could, I had kept that hope alive. Still and all, his behaviors justified my worst fear.

In the end, it didn't matter how keenly I had tried to reach out to him. My efforts would always be reduced to a complete *échec*. The real tragedy in all this was that he had never tried to break away from that feeling of self-worthlessness.

Alas, my prayers could no longer be shield to his soul.

Albeit, most evils are acquired through indoctrination from early adoption of the Cardinal Sins, or perhaps simply the product of a chemical imbalance, the manner in which his actions were carried out suggested otherwise—Don's evil was innate.

He hated his life more than I could ever hate mine.

Until recently, I had always thought that nothing could come in between our friendship. From start to finish, I stood corrected.

I found myself the unwilling subject of betrayal. Don

possessed an unfailing ability to bring about mayhem on command, and for all my efforts I could not change that about him.

The damages were monumental, but at least the dissembled truth had been exposed. Our camaraderie should be a cause for celebration, not confrontation. Something was telling me that this conflict between us would not age graciously.

I battled to find peace, but nothing could extinguish the fire within. I felt evil rising steadily. No point of resisting.

No intention at all.

Chapter 19

Let it Burn

If things had changed, nothing had become better. Swiftly, the unlocked front door squeaked open, and in so doing, enabled an incursion by the foudroyant cold air inside all the rooms. Within the space of a frosty breath, the siege was complete.

It was an ostentatious custom-built five-bedroom hacienda that I had called home for little over a year now. The unusually immense backyard that caged two mourning willows in the far end was fenced by a sunset-colored brick wall. In proximity of the giants, sat a wooden gazebo with thatched roof that connected back to the patio by a chain-link of carefully emplaced nonagon stepping stones along the right side of the backyard. Next to the patio, a verdant Zen garden with a bridged pond occupied approximately two thirds of the entire area.

The real charm, however, was the motley assortment of wild roses, Scarlet Princesses contrasting with night blue hydrangeas framed in knee-high boxwood hedges that spread along the premises, and not to forget the climbing vines that crawled up the walls as veins that gave life to the house.

It was centuries ago.

From a lack of care, the tall weeds overlapped the beautiful rolling spread of green grass no longer existent. At one time, I proudly spent most of the evenings, when I was home, watering and caring for the overly abundant vegetation—a visually lush landscape once.

At the pinnacle of my own decadence, my life had become inexpressibly depressing. From one misery to another, I found myself in a state of limbo, incapable of letting go or moving on. On the other hand, what has not been subjected to any changes of sort was the persistence of my bad luck. My attorney called the night before with more artery-clogging news. The case would likely drag for years to come unless a miracle was to be ordained.

So many misfortunes had happened in such a short period of time that I felt compressed and mostly down-hearted. Inside my lonely mind, I projected against the dark screens of my closed eyelids images of my life, one mostly pummeled by hurtful memories and entangled now to the present only by harvestmen's webs.

If conventional wisdom considers a kernel of truth that nothing lasts forever, my irremediable suffering is evidence of that fallacy.

Following a squeak, I heard the patter of light feet approaching my bedroom in slow pace and rubbing against the porcelain tiles. The sentiment that it could've been a marauder left me neither alarmed nor frightened. Somehow, I recognized the synchronized taps made by those unique footsteps. Still, I bore no interest in speculating.

Then my bedroom's door swung open. As soon as it did, the faint corridor light vagabonded in, unannounced and most certainly unwelcomed.

From the corners of my bulgy eyes, I perceived an indistinct shadow advancing toward me as my tired mind struggled to regain focus from weeks of sleep deprivation. However improbable, it could have well been a dream.

When the dark figure closed in, I finally distinguished my father's face against the ghostly glow. Standing godlike and still, he looked around, his gaze investigating carefully my bedroom, before saluting me silently with the slight hint of a forced smile. Quickly irritated by the tenebrous cubic room, he lunged past me and opened the curtains before planting his feet next to the window as if to draw me in the direction of the light.

It had been a while since I'd seen daylight.

Motionless, I was sitting on the floor in the middle of

unfolded cardboard boxes, a phalanx of old newspapers towers piled asymmetrically, and a graveyard of empty bottles. My warzone-like house would have revivified the ruins of Pompeii back to its glorious days. But at that point, I cared not one bit.

If this was rock bottom, it felt more like six-feet under.

Having spent my last dime on the case, I had been courteously evicted. That was my last day in my own home, yet I had not packed much. Even the roaches had relocated from starvation. Too proud to ask for help, my only option left was to share habitat with the flies in my van. On the bright side, this self-inflicted punishment could be interpreted as a valuable lesson. On the condition I survived the ordeal, of course.

A broken heart is surely a slow agonizing death sentence.

My father was known to be a man of few words, but his short discourses always commanded respect. And though I clearly lacked the presence of mind I knew that he had something of a shut-up-and-listen importance to share with me.

The old man rarely visited. Thus, I owed him the decency to listen, at least with one good ear. Reputed to be mulish, I had the unmistakable impression that he wouldn't let go of me until he got what he came for. And this made me want to take a long peregrination into oblivion.

Fifteen years ago my knees would have shaken by such a visit. Now I was just a bit surprised.

This promised to be a long day.

Resplendent in his suit as usual, he seldom left the house without his fabulous shades. When I was growing up, most of my friends were intimidated by his quiet but well-felt presence, and especially his deep stare. In addition to his proud postures, the trench coat earned him the prominent status of a mob boss which I'd learned, in my nerdy years, to use to scare off bullies.

In a slow movement, I nodded in assent and leveled up my stare to his chin out of respect but dodged his eyes from fear of showing weakness under my skin, one troubling side of mine under extreme pressure. If at all, I was more ashamed perhaps of the way my life had turned out than of my barbaric appearance. Semiconscious at best, I ran my hands over my face to wash off the solidified vomit from the corners of my mouth to preserve that last piece of dignity remaining. But, even if I tried, I couldn't rid of the fetid stench from my weeks-long unwashed clothes.

It did not matter. I was suffering from a severe case of emotional vacancy, and nothing could shake me off anymore nor could it relieve that awful feeing inside.

Nothing.

"My son…" His voice trembled with emotion and trailed off before he finished the sentence, "…don't live in despair, it will destroy you."

"I know, Pa," I muttered after a brief moment.

"I'm sorry if I wasn't there to help you through your struggles and—"

"Don't worry, I understand your reasons," I interrupted him. Then something triggered in me, a need to express myself after a lifetime of silence. I might never get that chance again, I figured. Without holding back as never before, I peppered him with a flurry of questions. "Where were you all my life? Do you know that I learned to ride my first bike from a stranger? Do you know that? Do you?"

It was then that he approached me with teary eyes, put his hands on both my shoulders, and stooped at my level, showing the despairing concern of a parent at the side of a dying child. It was the first time that I witnessed that beautiful man cry.

"I am sorry," he said in a conciliatory tone. "I wish things could have been different between us, but I'm afraid I cannot mend the hurt I've caused all of you. I'm truly sorry, son. But today I am not here to talk about the past. I'm here to talk about your future. And I think you will find my insight valuable."

A long broody silence swept in. We rarely had any father-son moments, and so the situation became quickly awkward and tense on both ends.

Without waiting for any answer, he went on, "I am here to prevent you from doing things that would make you scared of yourself in retrospect when your mind is clear again. Life is but a choice."

"What are you talking about?" I retorted with an elevated voice.

In a peremptory orotund voice, à la Morgan Freeman, as if to restore order, he replied, "Son, I think that you are too smart for what's happening to you."

"I'm not quite sure I follow!" I puzzled further.

"Do not take me for an imbecile! You know exactly what I'm talking about! I know that it has crossed your mind once too many times!"

For an instant, there was another bone-chilling silence.

"Listen!" he added. "I have encountered numerous people in my lifetime who wished me harm, but I chose not to retaliate in any way."

I remained quiet as he went on with a piercing monologue.

"Don't become one as your deceiver. You must forgive Don and remember that he was your friend once. So keep the good memories and move on. You have to let it go, because that's the only way. Don't make an all-in wager with the devil for I'm afraid you would be destroyed ultimately. There is no satisfaction and found-glory in hatred." He paused to catch his breath and added, "No sons of mine, while I'm still alive, will surrender to evil. I know that just as I have, you live in your own little world. I'm aware of that, but the difference is that I live in pacifist darkness, whereas yours is dangerously brewing. Once you enter the realm of bitterness, there is no turning back."

After a quiet moment, just when my father thought that he had broken into my thick skull, I sprang to my feet and demanded, "What about my sufferings? What about all the lies? What do you make of all that?"

"Calm down, my son. I don't recognize you anymore. You are getting uglier by each word of hatred."

Another pause.

"In time you will feel better, and this whole mess will just be a freight of bad memories. Believe in the power of time, and your wounds will heal. I promise."

"I can't! It's stronger than me! Besides, he drew first blood!" I retorted angrily with no signs of abating.

"This I cannot allow, my son!"

"So what? I should just let it go?

"*Yes,* precisely! Don't worry about your pain. It will go away someday. Most important, don't give in to hatred because in nuance it will never go away and your failure to make the right choice will only perpetuate your suffering."

To which I countered, "Forgiveness is for the weak. That's what people feed those they hurt out of fear of retaliation. And why should I be the only one suffering?"

"Wrong! Only through forgiveness will the suffering stop. You are just too involved with yourself in this anger affair to see clear."

"So there isn't any justice for me ultimately?" I replied.

"On the contrary. Taken from experience, you'd rather be the one hurting than the one inflicting the pain. Believe me, you have a far better deal. Someday the pain will shift to him and it will stay there permanently. You must always remember that even in situations such as this, it is through moral virtue that sanity itself lives on. All that matters is that you have been a good brother to him. And don't worry about receiving any gratifying moral fees. Your kindness is the real reward."

Following this strong philosophic disagreement, another silence reigned.

"Bottom line, you have to let it go. Your blame is misplaced. Don is not Lucas. He could never replace Lucas. And that's your mistake to think otherwise and to fancy his life. It's time to live your own!" He cleared his throat and concluded, "If not for you, do it for your daughter."

Despite the solemn reality that we didn't have much of a history together, I was speechless, again, whenever my father gave me sagacious advices, as infrequent as it was. After the moral audit, it became evident that the bitterness was killing me faster than the pain itself, and the price to pay would cost me more than what I had lost at this point.

My soul.

As hard as it was to divorce the man from his actions, slowly the image of Mephistopheles dissipated inside my mind until I recognized Don's face again, the face that reflected once upon friendship. Circumstances being what they were, I would only retain the glorious phases of our brotherhood and expurgate everything else.

This had been the longest conference I ever had with my father in my entire life. His words were of monumental meaning, although it is one thing to understand and widely another to put those information into full use.

Having gone through an emotional quake, I suspected the aftershocks ahead would be nothing less substantial, which I must discover for myself. This was just the tier of the storm.

Greater challenges lay ahead.

Chapter 20

What's Love?

For the last three hours or so, all I could feel was constant sharp stings of pain in my abdomen. Incapacitated by a wave of nausea, there was little chance I would recover anytime soon, if at all—the odds were almost negligible. At some point, the pain metastasized in pinball fashion between my sternum and lower back.

It was the fifth time this had happened in recent months, but tonight the pain was mercilessly vindictive. In leaps and bounds far greater than anything I had experienced before, it would not renounce its quest for doom.

For the first time, and surely not the last, the intensity had become more than I could bear—a trip to the ER was imminent. I have always been very circumspect to tread upon this path but before this newly severe case of sudden breathlessness by contrast, I couldn't afford to ignore the obvious anymore. Intuitively and perhaps unyielding to defeat, I felt confident I would survive the drive to the hospital before I passed out.

The concept of time, and everything else, ceased to matter.

Is this the end? I had never before given so much thought to the possibility.

At the ER, the L-shaped waiting area was filled far beyond its maximum capacity with mostly elderly folks and children all suffering from influenza, the soup-du-jour. More patients flocked in behind me as I bustled pass everyone and settled on the floor in front of the line, groaning and panting.

Never one with talent to normally draw a crowd, I was the cynosure of all eyes. No adjectives could have described the pain. Murderous, at best.

The medical staff took me in immediately after I started rolling on the ground and screaming. As some might allege theatrics to get ahead by the look in their hypothermia-cold stare, they would be within their rights, but wrong. Most of the kids were terrified, and the younger ones cried from the brouhaha I caused.

Abetted by a sense of insouciance, I liberated myself from morals and ethics selfishly. I did not have a care in the world considering the general attitude of the day—a few people I would have even wished this pain upon blatantly, given the opportunity.

I feared no judgment.

Honesty should never be a crime. At the end of the day, all that mattered was that I did more good than harm—a motto I've adopted for a while now.

It worked so far.

For the first time in my life, I was not suffering from a prolonged emotional wound. After imploring so long for this transition to find assuagement from my heartbreak, the change was disappointedly unwelcomed. The pain would not give me the satisfaction.

Careful what you wish for, I realized a bit too late.

Soon after, I was put in a room subdivided into three sections by shabby dark green curtains halfway-shut. The only bed available was situated at the end of the room. The sheets were newly replaced and infused with the fainted aroma of disinfectants which made me doubly queasy.

Next to me, a gray-haired woman with an empty face was sobbing and sniffing sporadically. "After a lifetime together, my hubby left a year ago on Christmas Day," she kept on saying. "He's abandoned me for no apparent reason."

To my relief the tone of her thunderous voice dramatically hushed down to a murmur. "Whatever happened to *For Better or For Worse, In Sickness or In Health*? No such thing as love, you live and you die alone, that is all!" she said in a painful breath.

Judging by this melodrama, I reckoned other factors at play leading to the old man's estrangement, but I opted wisely to adopt silence owing to the sensitivity of the situation.

On the third bed, a fifty-something Hemingway aficionado with a rusty-bedraggled lumberjack beard whose first intention was to regale our little group with elevating anecdotes offered to make a prayer for her.

To which the old lady segued, "Thank you, dear, but beliefs only lead to blind faith and God has left this place long ago. He and my Joel once loved me truly. Now there's only pain."

"God is merciful, but I am not sure, he'll meet Him at all," the man yelled out.

But his attempt at ingratiating himself with her failed to gain traction and only fueled her frustration further. The very suggestion was more than she could endure for it was but of a shadow and remembrances of past that she clang to now. Even my worst days would pale against what she was going through.

As it turned out, being alone was not that appealing, after all.

Before her self-pity behavior became all the more pronounced again, I succumbed merrily to the morphine. Slowly adrift, my consciousness began to wane. I could hear their conversation tamped down in distant echoes until everything fell quiet

A reprieve much needed.

When I emerged from oblivion, the old lady was gone and so was the protracted pain. "She was dismissed at her own request excoriating that she had had her fill of temporary fix," the nurse, a petite redhead with a *jolie* face, answered after I inquired of her whereabouts for small talk. Then she added, "Don't mind her. She's mostly here for an audience. Tonight was her second admission this month alone. She laments her lost love more than her pain."

A bit odd a statement, but it rang some truth, which explained why the old lady was not cared for with great concern. After tending to all my capricious demands, the nurse exited the room leaving behind a trail of lavender scent, and a dreamy smile—the kind that would nurse any wounded soul back to health.

I was alone.

The room was cold.

I had left my sweater in the car to my regret.

The old woman had dealt the coup de *grâce* to all my hopes. Maybe she was just a mercurial character of epic proportion from one end to the other, though I put no credence into that theory. It was hard to tell given the fatigue and the drowsiness.

In noctambulous mode, I waded through the dullness of the remaining of my stay under the assumption, for self-assurance, that there was a version in which I may be able to go home and live the life as I knew it.

My wonderful lonely life.

Before long, two male nurses of Penn and Teller's size proportions wheeled me to a faraway location where they took X-rays of my abdomen. Suddenly, my desire to unveil the truth was at odds with my fear of the truth.

Then silent radio.

Time crawled by.

Hour after hour after falling in and out of consciousness, the result finally came in—I was diagnosed with *calculus of gallbladder with acute cholecystitis*, or simply put in the vernacular, gallstones.

Everything else appeared normal, I was told, but without further testing procedures nothing was of certainty. Hypertension being the main culprit, however. *At least the news did not confirm my worst fear,* I thought.

"Stop boozing," the doc warned me plainly.

With that stance, there was nothing left to say.

When I came home late into the night something started to stir inside. Something that kept me wide awake long into my solitude. The weight of the old lady's words pressed down on me and had impacted me deeper than I admitted.

A sense of helplessness gripped me as the silence grew loud. It was inutile to quell the rising panic inside, her hopeless cries had effected a revolution in my mind.

Right before the auroral lights, the dying embers of this colorful night allowed me, a self-admitted contrarian, to catalog my inner thoughts and refute my own disbelief of the existence of true happiness. The very question of life and death was in full display. But they were not the focal point to my awakening.

It was love rather.

What's the merit of living without it? Perhaps, it's time to take a chance again. But I would not careen head-on into this obscure subject this time around.

Which begs the question: What's love?

Alas, from a lack of funding or should I say scholarly relevance, I assume, love has never been documented by science, or any other establishments for that matter, to the same degree unicorns have been by mythology.

An Area 51 sort of mystery it remains.

Back to reality, some clever minds believe that love is action—a concept that could have well been formulated out of a think tank conference. Pause for laughter. I disagree. My whole life, I have made sacrifices and always tried to accommodate people without expectations, but in the end, all I found was betrayal and deception. The reason being, people rarely take into account the kind gestures. It's all about what more can you do for them, for beneath the veil, we are but unrepentant savages.

Others postulate that love is the best represented by understanding. Pause for effect. Again, surely not. My opinion isn't an exact science but understanding is only possible through communication, as well as for trust, respect and so on. In that sense, all those terms, as single cell, cannot define love. They belong to a whole network of definitions, and each of them relies on the others to create a conjugation but never can they encompass love within their reach.

In some cases, love is mistakenly associated with the fear of being alone. Frightening as it may be, *forever* is indeed a long time to spend alone. Yet, when two people share a lifetime together out of emotional necessity, make no mistake, it's never about love.

It's called a settlement.

Interestingly enough, why are we afraid to be alone when we can fully function as one? And most important, why do we always allow our fear to commit treason against our reason? If only we were to give love a minor definition, to lessen its psychological impact and its intensity of which cannot fully be calibrated, such as satisfaction with the simpler pleasure of companionship, then I suppose happiness would not be too farfetched.

At issue is whether the relationship reaches full fruition, it creates attachments and co-dependency in forms of emotions and spiritual connectivity which in turn contribute to pain when all falls down. It's just the way life happens sometimes without any control on our part.

Today, by admission, we live in a different world where love is underrated, where it's easier to leave, and marriage not so symbolic an institution anymore but an anticlimactic affair full of empty promises, without any real meaning of substance.

Misguided hope can be heavy a burden to bear when

we cannot bring ourselves to be the right person by way of compromise.

Above all, what's deeply concerning is that people would so willingly surrender to the idea of being complete *only* with someone which, forgive the arrogance, is an affront that renders the notion of self-importance as a footnote. Whoever may rebuff this verity would only be deluding themselves out of psychological necessity.

To cement this compilation of thoughts, love is unique in that it has always combined our individuality with a desire to unify with a significant other while completely ignoring the fact that soon or later that very individuality would manifest its independence.

In a court of public opinion, this by far would be the single most probable cause to a relationship fallout.

So what is really love? Is love the pulse of life? Or is it just a momentary fix to make our journey all the more enjoyable?

After exploring much option, perhaps love is simply to give freely even when the heart does all the thinking to the exclusion of logic or common sense. While the truth is a matter of conjecture, love, at least for my part, cannot be given a blanket definition for the simple fact that it is not meant to be defined but felt only.

On this end, I don't have the slightest clue nor do I care to find out anymore. I just want to feel it again and again without comprehension. No matter how many times I would fall, I would get up and ask for more love hoping that at some point I will get it right. Practice may not make it perfect but experience would surely make it easier.

And so, if the brain cannot stop the heart from aching by way of intellectualization, then it is not the most powerful tool we possess.

The heart is.

Why people always think otherwise, I am not sure. This is the sort of question that would certainly warrant degrees of compelling extrapolations. Be that as it may, you may not find love until you start looking not by sight but soul, and treasures you shall uncover—a constant menu to feed my new *raison d'être* henceforth.

While the hamster that runs the wheel in my head has lost steam on this narcoleptic subject, I will settle for this. Perhaps my little nephew Henry, whose young age being a badge of innocence and honesty, defines Love best when he had his first crush: "It's Love because my heart sings aloud boom-boom!"

This would be a good place to begin.

Chapter 21

O L'Amour!

In the implicit view of the great Saint-Exupéry, flying gives us a sense of entitlement, of being godlike even within our own right. That elevating metaphor, aside from the ethereal element, stuck with me as part of the cultural heritage I'd received early on. More than accounted for, the aeronaut's words resonated in my psyche whenever I was pitted against darkness—to remind me, it seems, that there's something beyond the human understanding abutted to an intellectually unjustifiable absolute faith.

Decades later and by then an unfulfilled man in a midst of a creative drought, for the most part, I had a less glorious interpretation of that notion. I loathed flying.

The doc told me that my heart could not withstand deep underwater pressure much less high altitude. I would be courting high risk in those milieux, he cautioned. But that wasn't the real issue. More than anything else, I detested the idea of being confined.

Case in point, while on a voyage bound to Paris, the armrest-hogging barefooted troglodyte next to me only reinforced my disdain for flying. The worst part perhaps, was that he ran his mouth the entire time to anyone willing to listen. Eight hours of sleep deprivation until the final destination.

As soon as I set foot on the surface of the Hexagon, my olfactory receptors missile-guided me to the nearest food court to indulge a large *quiche au gruyère* and two servings of Parisian flan. I was famished, having given away the airplane convection-oven-heated-jail-style food to my neighbor in exchange for a moment of peace.

Everything had that familiar feel to it, everything but me. I was the blemish in the masterpiece. After such a long time in voluntary exile, I returned a changed man. Napoleon never had that chance, the poor man.

While it took a moment to adjust to the constant chattering of that romantic language, it felt as if I never left. To my amazement my French was intact, sort of, and so was my overly-pronounced southern accent.

My first day back offered a rose-tinted view of the past. The childhood's memories carried abroad all these years summoned a feeling of nostalgia for the good old days, at the crossroads of cultures.

I was home.

Under the restraint of parenthood, I only had five days to enjoy my stay, the sixth being an all-flight back. The whole and sole purpose of this short trip was a surprise visit to Lucas's mother—misdeeds of the past that needed correction. Almost every day for nearly two decades now, I've kicked myself for not coming sooner.

On the second day, while having chocolat-au-lait with Aunt May, someone entered the room and took the element of surprise from my unannounced visit and turned the table on me.

It was Lucas's long lost fiancée.

Who would have thought? I had not been there half an hour.

A cosmic coincidence would be appropriate a description.

At the very sight of me, she dropped her handbag from a nervous gyration and stood still, eyes all aglow, mute as a wax sculpture of herself. Because of the hair, I did not recognize her at first glance. Time, depression, and whatever else, all contributed to her meteoric aging. She approached me with teary eyes and made me wish, at that moment, I had not come.

Two decades had gone by, gray and blue and dark, but it seemed that it was just a moment ago. As I found out, after Lucas's passing she'd moved in to care for his mother—and never left. It turned out, ironically, if not for Aunt May she would have advocated euthanasia to end her own misery. That she survived his death and made the most out of her life seemed extraordinary enough, but equally remarkable is the tenacity of her resolve to stay the course.

As dictated by fate, the decision to remain with Aunt May saved her—complicity saved them both apparently—and brought a sense of closeness to him, she explained.

"We both struggled to find peace, but I knew that it was twice as hard for her. No parent should carry the burden of burying their child." She paused to wipe her tears. "Being together to confront our mutual loss gave us the strength we desperately needed."

And that was enough to go on. They had fed on that warmth and it made the days go by with more ease. It comforted me to see that they had managed well in my absence.

For anything, I was the one that needed saving.

Her natural color returning to her cheeks, she could hardly control the emotional impact tremor and cried as soon as she realized it was really me, in flesh and bone. The inconsolable weeping of a mourner has always spooked me. Another reason I stayed away all these years. She re-opened old wounds by adding more salt on what was pacified ages ago.

Or was it?

Before I could protest, Aunt May apologized for not

telling me sooner about their coalescence from fear that I might have run off again. "Forgive me, my son. I should have told you, but I thought that you two could use some closure also."

She knew me all too well.

I was ashamed of myself, and tried to cope with the numbness of shock at best I could. Any effort for an admission of guilt would not formulate into words, even if I tried.

Given the jet lag and the fatigue, it took more than a breath to absorb what was happening. It is worth noting, however, that no amount of preparation could have readied me for this. I had lost touch with them for so long in this epochal struggle, I was not aware that she never married. A part of her had ceased to exist. Most people would have moved on, but she was not most people.

Her heart had remained loyal to Lucas, the long-departed love of her life.

We stared long at each other as if to ask for emotional permission to unlock that painful door again. The splendor in her eyes still radiated that gentle kindness. I had not forgotten the bigger-than-life look inside, the same that sparked once in Lucas's forever gone now.

No one said anything for some time.

The silence broke when her eyes followed mine on one of the pictures on the wall, one unspoiled by time that I had no distinct recollection of its existence showing the three of us by the ruins of a monastery. I longed desperately to recapture those *Auld Lang Syne* moments but not one memory came to mind. I was left more baffled than I had ever been.

The chubby ugly little kid in that picture was probably six, my best guess.

After all this time, the only subject was Lucas. We did not talk much about anything else. Time did not heal our suffering after all. In this instance, we did not allow it to do so.

Woven in between memories in search for catharsis she sobbed some more, Andrea Bocelli playing·softly in the background. In me she saw a wraith of him, she muttered, the sound of her voice barely detectible. More than she had ever wanted anything, her only regret was not having children with Lucas.

How does one respond to that? I struggled to articulate my thoughts.

Unable to say and do anything of use, I feigned toughness.

I needed to be a rock for her. One of us had to be strong, and that would not be her. Weakness is a plague and would not go away easily. After all these years most people would have changed, but we were not most people.

As the crimson evening sky slowly darkened above, I implored her to let go of Lucas once and for all but fell short in my comment. That little voice inside condemned me for being hypocritical and unconscionably sanctimonious. How dare you decry her mourning while ceaselessly courting yours internally? It reproached me.

Blank, shame-faced, tar and feather—the whole nine yards.

Nothing I could say would matter. Against the certainty that she had already made up her mind long ago, my inputs were unnecessary. She would not resign to defeat nor accept that it was all that life had to offer. She knew something else greater was in the making. So she conspired silently an escape, and waited with resolve—the kind that could break or make a person.

Trying desperately to keep a straight face, I took a sip of the *Thé de Tilleul au miel* to flush in the last piece of *Crêpes aux fraises à la crème Chantilly* to clear my throat. I was hiding my feelings. Experience had polished my skills well in these matters when need be. I had not cried much in years, but it was hard to contain my emotion that day.

Cast from the same mold, the story of their life had become a tale of enduring love, one of the few of such unembellished stories that have always fascinated those whom they've touched at some point as much as those whom love had not yet struck with truth.

A demure little woman, I have long thought of her to being a prisoner of her own conscience where happiness belonged to a figment of the past, but this was far from fact. It was an act of love, pure and simple.

All these years had gone by, but still the flame of devotion burned brighter than ever. Nothing seemed to break her capacity for hope, all of which seemed to rest on the premise that their love would survive anything.

And it did.

In all my years, I never felt anything so otherworldly powerful.

Living in a dimorphic state, her body was soulless, but her love for Lucas was very much alive. In such close proximity, I could almost discern the intensity of the raw energy that fueled her will. Witnessing this beforehand gave me hope that someday someone would love me with the same truth and devotion.

The constant sinner in me was envious of their love.

The Heavens might've suggested an alternate life, less painful, but she remained true to herself. One thing was irrefutable. She represented, through the embodiment of quiet strength, love itself, the kind I was unable to express and would never for that matter.

Far removed from any doubt, she found solace in that death, the instrument of her damnation, would also be the bridge to liberation. On that note, she's paced her days under the tutelage of faith assailed by the sincere belief that their love was the irrevocable product of divine providence, and that in due time, they would be awarded an eternal life of abundance as soul mates.

After a much needed pause, I extended my hand to her in silent apology. In the center of my palm sat the wedding ring that Lucas had personally designed for her.

She'd never before seen it because I unknowingly took it with me abroad all these years. That was the real purpose of this visit, to leave it in the care of Lucas's mother to do what she would of it.

In the end, the ring found its way back to its rightful owner.

Contrary to what I initially assumed, this was not a chance meeting but had kismet written all over it. As she dabbed at her tears with a mouchoir, she murmured, "Given the pain and the loneliness, if I was afforded the choice, I would not change a single detail."

That's what love is.

Chapter 22

Alate

Today, unlike every other morning, the heat becomes intolerable inside the van. The positioning of the scalding San Joaquin valley sun shows noon and by now the tempests of the hangover have grown calmer. My eyes, no longer emblazoned by the sundry shades of gray, are introduced anew to the pastel colors of life.

Not a cloud in sight.

Despite my strength being wrung from me, I gather what's left of my humanity and my will. After suffering such a macabre psychotic episode in solitude, one would have surrendered their soul willfully.

Astonishingly, I thrive.

Something in me refuses to be hurled into eternity, just yet. For the very first time in many lunar cycles, there is a pulse to my life. Most people would call it a glimpse of hope. I beg to differ. Hope alone without the intended change is prerequisite to failure.

I prefer to call it a sweating cartridge-deprived compartment of the Russian roulette.

As I get up, I feel heaviness in my stomach, the sort that would not let go easily without a last fatal blow. Not for a minute has the depression been a magnanimous adversary, but at least I am still alive.

Ostensibly.

At breath's end, I recollect my thoughts from the reverie, and it dawns on me that there are a few too many discrepancies between my reality and, well, reality. Insofar as it can be ascertained, it took a sojourn in purgatory to comprehend that Don's enmity and my relationship fallout only amount to a minor fraction of the issues that have subtracted harmony out of my life.

For decades long I have functioned under the effect of the pain without concrete certitude of the underlying dynamics. But as of late, the urge for self-preservation and a once-latent desire for truth are showing peaks and troughs again.

More appropriate to the facts, the real tragedy is lodged deeper in my past and has endlessly controlled my emotions and my line of thoughts for the major part of my existence. All doubts set aside, the eruptive rage inside had been indeed incurred earlier than presumably thought. If anything, my childhood should have been blissful and filled with loving people, but that's not exactly what happened. While most kids my age collected trophies and awards, I was the recipient of painful memories, a mind full.

From the first encounter with fear, at the hands of the Minotaur, all my sense of *joie de vivre* had been detained in a solitary confinement. That occurrence, in part, had set in motion a locomotive of trauma. Following my head-on collision with the pain, any taste of life suddenly had no more appeal. I had drifted so far off from reality that all the lies I'd told myself became plausible, if not entirely believable.

Usurped by a myriad of suffering I withdrew into my inner sanctuary, the comfort zone—the last stronghold for peace of mind.

It was then that I began to harbor doubts that my life would ever get better.

What remains true to this day is that I feel as if I still have the instincts of that frightened little kid who more than anything longed for a dignified normal life. Deep inside, I've never stopped being that chubby ugly little kid.

All I wanted was to escape my suffering, but never was I given the tools. Alas, when the emotions constantly confirm defeat something has to give, in this case, a whole systematic shut down of my entire being. As I fell apart, all that's left afterward was a feeling of self-worthlessness.

Not surprisingly, the punishment did not stop with the abuse. Along the years, the trauma bred offspring of depression, as the situation swerved into a turbulent downward spiral.

In the long human struggle, victims of abuse rarely heal in full capacity as their life energy exudes out of their being in slow-released agony. Of course, such sacrilege was never part of any of my plans, and I wonder if the big guy up there, if in fact there is one, knew anything about it. While part of me avows the fault not mine hence an act of penance unnecessary on my end, another part isn't convinced I would entirely recover from childhood.

In the wake of the traumas, my whole being had been reformulated to react with unappeasable anger to any deception and torment. And so, whenever I felt unimportant or expendable, that programmed-reaction automatically re-emerged. As far as memory can stretch, I became the shadow of the person I was supposedly born to be, before the anger. From a distant reality, I hated myself not knowing better that my original being had long since vanished into obscurity.

Without my conscious awareness, that other person in me has been siphoning the very essence of my humanity. I am trapped in a life that holds no merits unless I reverse the effects of the self-destructive behaviors that had plagued my existence thus far. Depression, despair and self-destruction are in fact a whole network pertaining to a formula prescribed for a suggested catastrophe.

Years of eventful unrests can tear apart even the most resilient of souls as trauma becomes tradition.

At this stage of my life, I'm not quite sure which hurts more, the pain or the realization that I have lived a lie all along. Up until I came face to face with my mortality, I have always been living on the safe side by dodging the truth. But lately, with faith in short supply, the tapestry of my life is unreeling its last threads a fiber away.

In this final hour, I will not stray from reality.

Odd as it might sound, logic deducts that I am the last substantial, but not insurmountable, obstacle to my own happiness—lest we forget, the fiercest opposition comes from the devil inside. A tour de force is undeniably indispensable to compartmentalize truth from fiction.

For the present, I can't help but admit in complete honesty that Don's banditry to my humanity is insignificant, just a particle of grime in my quotidian struggles. Against my better judgement, I am my very own worst enemy.

Too many red flags have been raised to ignore the imminent threat the anger poses. To say the least, the anger, no longer at its infancy stage, has reached the upper echelon of intensity. Those facts about my past, as vexatious as they may be, are finally brought up to light and require an urgent intervention.

Excuses after excuses, I have always been afraid to

look inside my darkness knowing well that only a spiritual voyage into that most terrifying place would unravel the spring of this ever-growing pain. Sometimes everything needs to be leveled to dust in order to rebuild—even if change can be a scary place to wander about. Still and all, only the cowards would remain and torture themselves dwelling on "what might've been."

Today, by exemption, I will no longer look into the face of memory nor reprise the role of the victim again. For too long I have lived in denial and set my problems in suspension. By such deeds, I have come to believe their existence a matter of the past. Was I so wrong?

They had taken roots instead. Deeply.

As verification to that truth, my reaction to my heartbreak could have been less heightened if the ensemble of traumas amassed from childhood had not been as severely embedded in me. Unequivocally, such reaction was an aberration exaggerated out of proportion.

It all started with the yearning for a mother's affection that I did not fully receive during early childhood, which later became the driving force that had gradually pushed me on the brink of the abyss. My kryptonite-attachment to my mother had held me hostage both psychologically and emotionally—the invisible umbilical cord had never been severed.

One after the other, I had projected that craving of what I took to be love onto every women that I had inter-developed some sort of bond with. Out of sheer ignorance, I was moving from my mother's nest into another woman's safe haven unable to break away from anyone who had shown me affection and acceptance. But reality is the void could have not been filled by external factors. These reasons explain the insufferable nostalgia when letting go of what's dear to me, whether it be the loss of a loved one or the dissolution of a relationship.

As I am living on borrowed time, the pain has exceptionally rained locusts on me, as though to stonewall any chance at recovery. To stop the self-inflicted apocalypse, I am in dire need of a spiritual innovation to shred the remnants of a dreary life I no longer wish to pursue.

My past can no longer excuse my failures. Being the epicenter of my own universe my recovery depends on the redefining of my true self—be the best representation of myself or become the exact opposite, the choice is mine.

The first step toward happiness starts with the respect of self. Everything else is frivolous remedial incantations that will sooner or later wind up in deception owing to the power of expectation.

Standing one inch away from losing ground with my sanity, it's high time to let the brain interfere and assert positive changes where the heart had failed. The mind alone should be the only locus of command in our life. Although, I must confess, we do not deserve stewardship of its power.

That little nagging voice inside is not to be ignored

anymore if the pillars of my reason are to be restructured. I have no intention of leaving any loose ends that might compromise this whole recovery operation.

Failing is absolutely not an option. I could not risk for my daughter to embark into the same vicious cycle and fall prey to depression. No matter the price to pay, I shall come out a victor, an entrepreneur of dreams even, and ride the tidal waves of life without fear or restraint. I would not allow my demons to be passed on onto her. She would become an exact replica of me in no time.

Life should not stop because someone betrays you, fails to appreciate you, or violates your humanity. Life should go on regardless of the circumstances. What matters is that I am able to walk away with a tranquil conscience. Sometimes being a champion is not necessarily about winning but to emerge a learned person at the very hands of defeat.

Today, I have come to terms with the pain. The madness ends here.

As soul-lifting as those findings may be, the excavation of my true self subsumes under another issue, something of immediate concern far too long mythologized in the subconscious. Much to my dismay, I also uncover that the traumas from childhood had created all along a much bigger problem whose effects are far more destructive than that of the anger itself.

In so many words, the fantasy in which I lived in had deluded my perception of reality and contributed to a coextending fictional world. From the moment that fear had been instilled in me, the trauma and the anger, acting as co-conspirators, had simultaneously robbed me of my self-worth. Subsequently, I lived in total dishonesty with myself. As the result, I adopted a self-mandated servile mentality to avoid being ostracized. If that wasn't enough, being distasteful toward myself, I was inclined to believe that my existence had only significance in the eyes of the outside world.

From an early age, I ensconced myself in the comfort zone to find protection from depression and trauma, never realizing that that very sanctuary had become a desecrated basilica of desolation, and more important, the direct cause to my inability to function independently in adulthood. In the course of the years, I had lost most of my social skills, if not all. And because I was suffering from an introverted emotional bleeding my life had only evolved within that virtual reality.

Under my unsuspected eye, the Comfort Zone has been all along the real demon.

All of these rationalizations explain my unwillingness to let go of Ali and Don because they imparted to the very core of my comfort zone, the only world I knew. When finally their betrayals provoked an internal implosion, the bubble burst wide open, and I was left for the first time to face reality alone.

For what's worth, I am thankful for the pain. Had it not been for its suffocating grip, I would have never recognized my real values. One cannot truly feel alive or appreciate life unless they've gone through the pain of losing everything and themselves in the process.

In any event, suffering does build character and more so becomes inspiration for change—nothing happens by hazard.

The gap between the ugly truth and the promise of a better life shortens by the moments as I recuperate from my emotional wounds. All the while being cautiously optimistic, it's time to clear some mental space to better recapture the simple capacity of thinking. There isn't anything more rewarding in life than shedding skins without losing the notion of self. Already, I can feel the void in my soul being filled steadily with an influx of harmonious energy.

This traverse into darkness to regain my footing has proven well-nigh impossible, but puissant again I feel by the moment. Today I am well aware that even the wisdom of a sage could have not set me free knowing that I hold the key to my own cell.

As popular conception may have held, our perpetual struggles are the undeniable proof of our existence. Despite our best intentions, we all face the same wrath at some point in life—some internalize it, and others display it—for we are but devout servants to our own ignorance. This is the common pattern I have come to accept without contestation.

At last, I am confident the journey to recovery has

reached the last steps as I finally stop living in the fictional world, the comfort zone. Gone are the days of these antiquated idiosyncrasies that I have once and for all abandoned.

Today, I condone to my own clemency and opt to live free of torments and anger. After nine long months of spiritual vacancy and emotional relapses, in the van, my father's words finally give me the impetus to move forward. I am not to walk the plank, just yet.

In arguably the darkest time of my life, I unearth my salvation which is none but self-love. Indeed, the greatest journey in life is measured by the distance in which one was born to be and the person one has become. Equipped with a notebook and my will in my arsenal, time is past due to leave the nest in pursuit of happiness—and fly away.

About the Author

Jess Lee Jalao currently lives in the Central Valley of California, where he helps individuals with developmental disabilities integrate into society in order to live as independently as possible. After years in this field, it was, in fact, those very individuals who have shown him that the true beauty of life lies in the simplicity of things, which, in turn, helped polish his writing skills.

He is almost never the most-educated person in the room, but don't anyone feel sorry for him. He speaks four different languages fluently, including Spanish and French, which are, as he puts it, lullabies to the soul. Having grown up abroad contributed to this motley of beautiful tongues.

At young age, Jess was introduced to many literary figures, including Antoine de Saint-Exupéry, Federico García Lorca, and Ernest Hemmingway, among other greats.

His affinity for the game of chess reflects greatly on his writing as well, and it makes perfect sense. His main character is always a few steps ahead, leaving the reader unaware, at times, of what's coming, and wanting to unveil the rest of the story while navigating through the twists and turns of the plot.

At night, when imbued in the solace of silence, he pours his passion into words and strives to appeal to the readers, all the while, respecting his individuality as a man of letters.